AT THE CORNER
—OF—
Magnetic
and Main

This book is a work of fiction. Any similarities to persons living or dead, or somewhere in between, is a coincidence. Even the town of Eureka Springs in this story and some events that take place there are a fantasized version of reality.

First Edition
Printed and bound in USA

ISBN: 978-1-942428-50-3

Cover design by Kelsey Rice
Formatting by Kelsey Rice

"There are more things
in heaven and earth, Horatio,
Than are dreamt of in your philosophy."

William Shakespeare
Hamlet, Act 1, Scene 5

Also by Meg Welch Dendler

Bianca: The Brave Frail and Delicate Princess

Cats in the Mirror Chapter Book Series:

Book 1: *Why Kimba Saved The World*

Book 2: *Vacation Hiro*

Book 3: *Miss Fatty Cat's Revenge*

Book 4: *Slinky Steps Out*

Book 5: *Kimba's Christmas*

And the Companion Books:

Max's Wild Night

Dottie's Daring Day

AT THE CORNER
—OF—
Magnetic
and Main

Meg Welch Dendler

P

Pen-L Publishing

Fayetteville, Arkansas

Pen-L.com

Chapter 1

Life never ceases to be life, just as love never ceases to be love, and love is eternally at the heart of what every immortal soul yearns for. The desire for love, the wrenching yearning for it, continues long past the grave. Penny had lost sight of those hopes and dreams over the years. Today, they would crash back into her life with a force that could not be ignored.

As Jake's motorcycle climbed steep hills and roared down the other sides, he knew it had been worth skipping work that day to take a drive. He reveled in the carelessness and freedom of the young, handsome, and uncommitted. His shaggy, brown hair blew in the breeze, and he stretched his fingers in his new, black riding gloves, working out the kinks in the tough fabric. There had never been a more glorious spring evening in the Ozark Mountains. Jake was sure of it.

The winter chill had given way to the first hints of warmth in the air. As the sun set, the sky blazed with orange-lit clouds. Violent thunder and lightning the night before had left the air fresh and clean and full of the promise of a new season. Damp, brown pine needles and soggy piles of decomposing leaves clung to the narrow shoulders of the road, not quite ready to admit that their time was done.

On this early spring day, Jake had toured all along Highway 62 through scenic biker routes, zipping past the centuries-old rock outcroppings that were the primary landmarks along the snakelike Arkansas mountain roads. He had just passed the creepy, giant ceramic bunny that sat—always watching—in a roadside front yard. It was an odd signpost, but it meant he was only thirty minutes from Eureka Springs. Even if it wasn't the official Pig Trail, an outstanding piece of highway lay before him.

Grown-up logic said that he should turn back to Rogers and head home, but the lure of the winding road ahead was a siren song he couldn't resist. Answering the call to adventure was easy to justify. He could simply extend the fun by spending the night at one of the easy-on-the-wallet biker hotels in the tiny, tourist town. There should be some good company and rowdy parties tonight with beer flowing freely. He had nothing to hurry home for and could always head back early in the morning. No harm, no foul.

That logic of the wild and free gave him the chance to take another run along his favorite stretch of road just ahead—daredevil, hairpin turns on a rocky mountainside where guardrails were scarce. The trick was to know when to brake, just at the last minute, to slide around each bend.

Barely budding trees overhung both sides of the two-lane road, their still-bare branches hovering expectantly around every curve. Jake leaned into the turns expertly, weaving within inches of the yellow center line as oncoming cars swerved away from his path. Dozens of bikers passed behind them, giving him a low thumbs-up or an imaginary high-five as they passed. He knew those comrades had just finished the epic turns and hillsides that were waiting for him. Blasting past the bright-pink warning of the "BIKER BEWARE" sign, he revved the engine and settled down on the seat in anticipation.

The next thing he knew, Jake was standing in an old-fashioned diner, staring at a bowl of ice cream on the bright-red counter in front of him. Confused, he looked up and noticed a brunette young woman standing on the other side of the counter. She had the most amazing green eyes he'd ever seen and was wearing what must have been a 1950s-themed uniform for the diner: her long, dark hair up high in a ponytail, a big poofed-up light-blue skirt nearly down to her ankles, a spotless white button-up blouse, and perfectly shined saddle shoes. She smiled at him, calmly, like it was just any old day of the week.

Looking around, Jake felt even more bewildered. This wasn't just any diner. He recognized everything. He had been here before many times when he toured along Highway 62 through Eureka Springs. Just last week, he and his buddy Ed had grabbed some burgers here before heading on to Mountain Home. Magnetic Ice Cream Parlor and Diner was a unique place. Delicious American home-style cooking pulled in tourists from everywhere in the world. The cobbler was amazing— tender, delicate, and flaky, like it was created by the most perfect grandmother in existence. He thought he could still smell the day's offerings wafting gently in the air, but it didn't bring him comfort now.

Jake stared blankly at the walls in front of him. As always, they were covered from top to bottom with fun Coca-Cola memorabilia—posters and antique Coca-Cola pictures, Coca-Cola mirrors and clocks, and dozens of vintage Coca-Cola advertisements. Even the wallpaper had Coca-Cola symbols from one end to the other. He'd never asked about it, but it was pretty clear that the owners had spent decades gathering every Coke item they could get their hands on. It gave the place a kitschy aura in a town that celebrated kitschy in every shop and restaurant. Today, for Jake, it was all just disorienting. The bright-red bottle caps swam in front of his eyes. Wasn't he just on the highway?

Adding to his confusion, there were no lights on in the diner. The place was usually lit up and bright and cheery, but now it was dark with only the slight yellowish glow from a clock nearby and the deeper, ominous red of the emergency exit signs.

He had been headed in to Eureka Springs, he remembered that, but it was dusk just a moment ago. The black windows beside him proved that it was now well past dark.

Did I stop by for dinner? Is the diner closed, and should I have left by now?

Looking back at the waitress standing serenely in front of him, his thoughts were even more scrambled. The old folks who ran this place didn't dress up in throwback costumes, and he most certainly would have remembered this pretty waitress with the green eyes.

Why is she just standing there? Am I supposed to order something or pay my check? I don't usually order ice cream. Why can't I remember?

He looked down at the untouched bowl of slightly melted chocolate ice cream on the counter and tried to put the pieces together, but none of it made sense.

How did I get here? he wracked his brain.

"Give it a minute," the waitress with emerald eyes said quietly. "It'll come back to you."

The light in the diner was dim, but as Jake looked around, he noticed that they were not alone. Two strangers sat at the bar to his left. They were both staring at him, expectantly. The young woman, wearing a fancy black-and-white maid uniform, smiled at him like he was a little child lost in a shopping mall. She tucked a wisp of curly, auburn hair behind her ear and crinkled her freckled nose in an anxious smile. The old man with crackly, black skin and bright-white hair smiled and nodded reassuringly. It didn't help. Jake just felt dizzy and even more confused.

He reached for the spoon in front of him to take a bite of ice cream. Maybe that would help. But instead of picking up the spoon, his hand passed right through it. He tried again in frustration, and then he felt the waitress's hand on his arm. Her touch had a strange, dreamy feel.

"It may not work just yet," she said.

The two others at the counter shifted uncomfortably in their seats.

"Miss Penny," the old man said, "ya best jus' tell 'im."

"It usually goes better when they can remember for themselves a bit first," Penny answered. "You know that much by now, Silas."

As Jake stared at the spoon and tried again to grasp it, the front door behind them swung open abruptly. Everyone at the counter jumped in surprise and turned to face it. Two older men, one in a robe and pajamas and the other in a police uniform, walked in and flipped on the front set of lights. No one at the counter moved an inch or uttered a sound.

"Thanks for opening up over here so I can use the phone, Hank," the sheriff said. "Hope we didn't bother Molly too much. That dang-blasted radio gets all kind of interference down here in the low parta town, and I let my damn cell phone battery run out again."

"No problem, Jimmy," the man in the P.J.'s said, yawning. "Must have been a bad one to get everyone up and moving this late at night."

"Yep," Jimmy said, starting to dial the red Coca-Cola-emblazoned phone on the far wall from the counter. "I guess they just found him. Crazy young fella must have missed the turn and *pssseeewww . . .*" He motioned with his hands in a large, diving arc. "Right off the edge of Highway 62 near Lake Leatherwood and into the trees a hundred feet below."

Hank shook his head sadly and wrapped his worn, plaid robe closer around him.

"I sure wish the state would put up a few more guardrails. Did he even have a helmet on?"

Jimmy just laughed.

"Not sure, but wouldn't have made much of a difference, from what I caught before the radio went out. That kinda wreck just leaves a big, gory mess. They're guessin' it happened earlier this evenin'. Kid actually went in the holler outside the city limits, but it seems like everybody took the day off today, goin' fishing and whatnot, so they're scramblin' 'round for help." His attention refocused on the phone call. "Yeah, Connie? Sorry we got cut off before. Did ya find any identification?" Jimmy continued, talking with the person on the other end of the phone.

But Jake wasn't really listening anymore. He realized that Penny was now holding his hand, and the two strangers at the bar had gotten up to stand right behind him, each with a gentle hand on one of his shoulders.

Something felt wrong. *Why can't I grab the spoon? Why are these people being so weird? And why don't those two men notice the four of us or say anything to us?*

It was like they weren't even there.

As his mind spun with questions, Jake heard his name. He looked up at Penny, and she smiled weakly, but it wasn't her talking. It was the sheriff.

"Jake Thatcher. Got it. Have you reached his family yet? Well, keep trying. Thanks, Connie." The officer hung up the phone and made a few quick scribbles on a notepad before tucking it into his jacket pocket.

"I'm Jake Thatcher," he said, breaking away from the counter and the supportive touch of the others there. "I'm right here."

Neither man reacted at all, like they were blatantly ignoring him. He remembered games like that on the playground at school. Everyone would pick one kid to ignore for the day. It was funnier back then.

"Well, Hank," Sheriff Jimmy said, "it sounds like they've got it all moving smoothly now. I guess you can head back next door."

"Hello?" Jake shouted, stunned by their stupidity or rudeness or whatever it was. "I'm right here!"

Neither of the men looked at Jake. They simply headed for the door.

Hank turned off the front bank of lights as Jimmy ambled outside, but Hank hesitated before leaving and glanced back into the room.

"Good night, Penny," he whispered. Then he locked the door behind him.

"What was that?" Jake demanded, mostly to the closed door and the two men who had left through it. He spun around and looked at Penny, then at Silas and the maid. "Are they dumb as rocks?"

"They can't see you," Penny said flatly. "They can't see any of us."

"But the guy said goodnight to you."

"Yes, well . . . it's complicated." She shrugged one shoulder. "But he didn't see me."

Jake went weak in the knees. Penny rushed over and helped him to the stool at the counter, but it felt odd underneath him, like it was soft and barely there.

"Why did that cop say my name?" Jake wondered.

Penny sighed. She looked at Silas and the maid and then leaned in close to Jake. She spoke slowly and carefully, as if she thought he didn't speak English very well.

"Sheriff Jimmy was getting the name of a young man who died in a terrible motorcycle accident today."

"But he said *my* name."

"Yes, he did," Penny admitted.

"But I'm not dead!" Jake shouted at her.

Penny squeezed her lips into a tight line and sat down next to him.

"I'm not dead," he said again, glaring at Silas and the maid. Silas looked at the ground. The maid just shook her head and wrung her hands slowly.

"So hard, so hard when they're young'uns," she said.

Penny leaned in close and whispered to him.

"Think. Close your eyes and try to remember."

Angry and frustrated, Jake tried to pull away, but Penny just held his arm patiently.

"Close your eyes," she said again. "Try to remember how you got here."

This time, Jake closed his eyes and wracked his brain. He'd been on his motorcycle, having an awesome time. He'd been flying around the mountain trails. He could remember zipping through what his buddies called the zombie pit—a spot where the road had been blasted right through a mountain that now rose up rocky and daunting on either side. They joked about how they could lure zombies there and block them in. Jake had buzzed through it going about ninety miles per hour. He could remember slowing down some for the tighter corners, careening past Inspiration Point and the Opera in the Ozarks building, but he had run the engine full out again across the bridge outside of town at Lake Leatherwood. A sense of pride swelled up, remembering he must have hit near one hundred on that flat stretch. But how did he end up in the Magnetic Ice Cream Parlor and Diner with strangers on the far side of the city at the corner of Magnetic and Main? Did he drive here? Was his motorcycle outside?

The cop had mentioned a terrible accident. The cop said Jake Thatcher had been in a terrible accident. But there hadn't been any . . .

Then—not all at once, like a scene in a movie, but in flashes of moments and feelings and images—Jake remembered. It sent an icy chill up his spine.

I didn't make that turn.

The road had still been wet in patches, especially on the shoulders. He'd seen the bright-pink warning sign miles earlier, but he hadn't slowed down. As if to spite it, he'd pushed on even faster, and then . . .

Yes, there had been a hairpin turn right past the entrance to Thorncrown Chapel. He'd leaned into it, but his bike had skidded off onto the wet, barely existent shoulder. He closed his eyes and let it all wash over him. There was a frantic moment when he'd realized that the bike was out of control—that slide and panic, his hands in the still stiff, new riding gloves, desperately clinging to his beloved bike as the wheels spun uselessly in the air—and as they had flown off the side of the mountain, he could see the forest lying below him, and . . .

Those men couldn't see me. They couldn't see any of us.

Dead?

Jake did not take the news well, but he did better than some. Penny and the others waited without comment while reality sank in.

Penny had been through this hundreds of times—stood at this counter, witnessed them suddenly arrive, served up a bowl of ice cream, and helped as best she could. Sometimes they moved on quickly, gone before saying a word. Other times, like with Jake and so many young ones, the transition didn't go so smoothly. It probably didn't help that this boy was handsome and still filled with adventure and life. From the look of him, he couldn't be much more than twenty years old. He was going to cling to what he had with all his might. It was written on every inch of him from his wild, brown hair to his black riding boots. Clinging and resisting would be dangerous. Even more dangerous than speeding along Highway 62 on a motorcycle.

Jake was different from anyone else who had passed through the diner. Penny could sense it the minute he appeared. She had learned that everyone has a life-force. If she was paying attention, she could feel it in the air around her. Jake had more of a life-tsunami.

Blam! His arrival had sent out a shock wave that vibrated right through Penny's whole being. She was grateful that he had been disoriented for a minute because it took her that long to regain her composure. From the startled looks they had shot in her direction, Katie and Silas felt it too.

Jake emanated freshness, vitality, and an overwhelming sense of masculine rebellion. No one would dispute the fact that the young biker was ridiculously handsome. There was no denying it. Penny had noticed it when he had visited the diner before. He may not have been able to see her then, but she had most certainly seen him. His charisma and charm enveloped a room the minute he swaggered in, and even a ghost sitting on the sidelines couldn't help but be impressed. But now that she was faced with his presence on the verge of moving on to whatever lay ahead, all of that was more of a liability than an asset.

Penny had a job to do. The anger and resistant energy bouncing off the walls of the diner had to be controlled and contained. A dish of ice cream, even the deliciousness of chocolate Blue Bell Ice Cream, might not be enough to get the job done this time. Penny needed to be calm, firm, and clear. Jake had been given a window of opportunity to adjust to his death, but she doubted it would last for long. This young man was going to need all the help she could muster.

Penny wished someone had been there for her when her time came. The night she had found herself standing alone in the middle of the dark diner had been horrible. That's one reason she had stayed there for so many years. Many lost ones passed through the door, and she knew she could be of some comfort. She knew she could help them adjust and come to terms with their totally altered lives.

Daytime in the diner was busy and full of life, but evenings were when those who could no longer truly enjoy the ice cream and cobbler came to visit. Silas and the maid, Katie, often stopped by. They had both been hanging around town even longer than Penny.

Silas was a convict who had died back in 1920 while working on building Highway 62 through town. He mostly hung out in a small cave below the road where the workers had slept, still wearing the gray jumpsuit with his prison number on the pocket. There was a thriving business there now, and lots of people came and went, but they couldn't see him. When he was lonely or bored, he wandered the quiet town after dark, meandered through Basin Park, or came to visit Penny.

Katie had been a maid at the Crescent Hotel back around 1900, when it was a really elite, luxury place to stay. She had accidentally fallen down the stairs, hurrying and carrying too much laundry at one time, and snapped her neck in an instant. That hotel was full of ghosts, human and animal, so she had plenty of company. There was a whole basement full of souls left behind by a quack doctor who ran the place as a bogus cancer hospital around 1940. Tourists came through every day trying to catch some evidence of a ghostly presence. TV crews had even set up shop, searching for proof of haunting events, forcing the no-longer-living to hide for days on end. Sometimes it all got to be too much. Once Katie found the peace and quiet of the comforting diner, she started visiting Penny regularly.

Now the three of them sat with Jake, sharing the worst moment of his existence. They had all been where he was now, and they knew there was nothing they could say to make it magically all better. Dead was just dead, there was no going back, and he was going to have to face it eventually.

In his rage and frustration, Jake had figured out how to bang the countertop with no-longer-material fists. Now he just sat in a crumpled heap, his head down on the counter, wrapped in his arms. Bit by bit, the frantic energy in the room began to settle and return to normal. *Maybe there is hope for this one after all*, Penny thought.

"Would you like to try some ice cream now?" Penny finally said.

Jake shrugged his shoulders without looking up.

"I'm afraid it doesn't taste as good as it used to . . . you know . . . before . . . but it's still nice."

Jake raised his head up slowly and rested it on one hand. Taking this as a "yes," Penny slid the bowl of partially melted ice cream in front of him. This time he was able to pick up the spoon and take a bite.

She's right, he thought. *Not as good, but still pretty good.*

It was familiar. Cold, sweet, and creamy. It was comforting. It made Jake think back on good times with his friends, right there in that very diner. After a long bike ride, they'd all stop in for the best burgers in town and some apple cobbler. Such a cheery place. They'd sit and joke about the old-fashioned ads posted here and there and try to count how many Coke symbols each wall held.

As he took a second bite, Jake noticed that Penny was getting a bit blurry. The whole room was. It was like he was looking at her through a smeary telescope lens. He shook his head, but that didn't help.

"Have another bite," Penny encouraged.

As he did, the room began to glow with a brilliant Light. Looking around in wonder, he noticed that Penny was smiling. Silas and Katie were smiling. Jake felt weak and weightless, but calm and peaceful at the same time.

What's in this ice cream? he wondered. The Light grew brighter and seemed to be focused directly on him. Panic rose up. *Wait a minute!* He knew what this was. He'd read enough books and seen enough movies.

"NO!" Jake shouted, slamming the spoon down on the counter. "I'm not goin' into any Light! NO!"

Immediately, the radiance ceased, returning the diner to an eerie semi-darkness. Jake sighed in relief. He felt like himself again, and he could see everything clearly, including the pretty green eyes of the waitress.

But her eyes had lost their sparkle, and she was no longer smiling. Her hands flew to her mouth, and she shook her head in horror.

"Oh, Jake," she whispered. "What have you done?"

Chapter 2

"This can't be happening!" Jake yelled. "I can't be dead! And I'm not going into any Light anytime soon, I can guaran-damn-tee you that!"

Penny scrunched her eyebrows, a sickening feeling spreading across her middle. What could she possibly say to him? It had been years since someone refused to go. The ice cream and the friendly place seemed to make them just slide on into The Light effortlessly. But Jake posed a unique set of circumstances.

At first, she was afraid The Light wouldn't even come for him. So much anger. But then it had started. His time had come, and The Light had spread effortlessly through the diner just like hundreds of times before. She had seen Jake start to fade and vanish into The Light, but then it was too late. He had slammed that door closed with a vengeance. Penny knew it might never open again. What could she possibly say to him to explain all of what that meant now for his warped sense of life?

She sat down at the counter next to him and folded her hands in her lap. It was easier to stare at her hands and hope for a miracle than try to explain what would happen now to this livid young man. Silas was not so hesitant.

"Boy, what'd you go'n do dat fer? You's stuck now," he said in disbelief.

Katie wrung her hands together harder and shook her head sadly.

"Oh dear, oh dear, oh dear," she whispered over and over. "I remember it like it was yesterday. So scared and so angry. Should have gone."

"What do you mean 'stuck'?" Jake asked Silas. Then he looked at Penny, her bright-green eyes still cast down. "What does he mean?"

"Just like us, Jake. Stuck here on earth."

"Maybe it's that I'm not really dead," he rationalized. "Maybe I'm just in a hospital somewhere in a coma or something, and if I fight hard enough, I'm going to wake up and this will all be a dream. It feels like a dream."

Penny just shook her head.

"That's not how it works. And besides, we heard what Jimmy said. Jake Thatcher is dead. They told the sheriff that right on the phone. You remembered the accident. You saw The Light come for you. Do you really think you are just in a coma somewhere?"

Jake stared at the huge, red, plastic Coca-Cola bottle cap on the wall behind the counter. No, in his heart, he knew that wasn't really true.

Dead? Stuck?

"I not sure dere be 'nough ice cream in da freezer ta covers tings up to-night, Miss Penny," Silas said. "You'd best makes him a cheeseburga."

Penny nodded and headed for the kitchen. Maybe Molly wouldn't notice if she cleaned up really well. The longtime owners of the diner never complained, but Penny liked to call as little attention to her constant presence in Hank and Molly's lives as possible—except when she was needed.

As Penny worked in the kitchen, frying up a juicy burger on the large, metal grill, Jake swiveled his barstool toward the stern face of Silas. Katie was still wringing her hands and fussing with her ruffly, white apron. Jake sensed he would get a straight and honest answer from the old convict.

"Okay," he said, "so what happens now?"

"Well," Silas shrugged, "dat fer yous ta figure out, I guess. I done been here fer over ninety years now an' just keep gettin' on from one day ta da next."

"Ninety years?"

"Yep, since da day I gots so drunk an' fell down dat big hill. We was workin' on buildin' da freeway. Da one ya just went a-flyin' offa. I had a bit too much ta drink a some moonshine we done cooked up an' fell an' hit my head. Reckon I hits it mighty hard. When dat Light come fer me, I didn' know what it was all 'bout. T'ought it was a car er somethin', an' I ran. Been stuck here eva' since."

"I was mad, like you," Katie joined in. "Fell down some stairs at the hotel because they made me carry too much at one time, and I couldn't see where I was going. 'Hurry up, Katie, now don't be so slow, lassie!' Humph. Cleaning up after me at the bottom of the stairs sure slowed things down for the night." She half-smiled and then dropped her eyes again. "So mad I wouldn't go either."

Jake glanced toward the kitchen.

"What about Penny?"

"She was sick. She was dying," Katie whispered, glancing hesitantly toward the red-and-white checked curtain that separated them from the kitchen area. "Her folks brought her here back in 1952, you know, for the water. That's what this whole town is built around. Even the natives way back thought the water here was magical. Fresh springs of water that will heal you. That's what they promised. Some even claim that it did. But not Penny. She had the cancer in her blood. There was nothing the doctors or the waters could do to save her, poor little thing. Not back then."

"But if she knew she was going to die, it shouldn't have been a shock. Why did she end up stuck?" Jake asked.

Silas and Katie exchanged glances, but neither had the answer.

Penny returned with a huge cheeseburger for Jake and poured him a large fountain Coca-Cola, so the conversation ended without conclusion. He sensed somehow that it was wrong to ask her outright about what had happened, so Jake just ate his cheeseburger in silence. The others were quiet too, keeping their own thoughts to themselves for the time being.

It was odd to still eat and drink, as if he were alive. It was the same in some ways, but vastly different in others. Jake could still taste and smell the food, though it was fainter than normal, like it was coming to him through a vast tunnel. But even odder was the fact that he didn't feel hungry when he started or full when he was done. That tender belly and deep satisfaction that usually came at the conclusion of a delicious meal eluded him. He did feel calmer, however, and more prepared to face what now lay ahead.

"I'm not sure why being stuck is so bad," Jake finally said. "That burger was great, and I feel fine."

"But not full, right?" Penny said. "Not satisfied."

"Well, no, not really, I guess."

"Eating brings emotional comfort, but you don't need to eat anymore. You don't really have a stomach. Ice cream is a big hit with the ghosts around here, but it's more about memories and a sense of home and family. That's probably the last burger you'll ever have much interest in. It's just not the same."

Jake looked down at his empty plate. The idea of never being interested in a big, juicy burger again was sobering.

"You don't need to sleep. You don't *need* to do much of anything," Katie added.

He touched the edge of the plate, tipping it from one side to the other.

"But why can I eat? I mean, if I'm not real, why can I make the plate move and eat the burger and sit on this stool?"

"It's all about interacting with the material world. It's much easier to keep behaving like you did while you were alive. You still have a kind of substance. You are still you, and you still have energy. What's hard is trying to take up the same space as something else—like moving through a wall. Work with material things, not against them."

Jake spun his plate around on the counter, and it clattered dangerously close to falling off the edge. Penny winced, putting her hand in the way, just in case.

"You can still break things," she said, setting the plate back in the middle of the counter. "You still see yourself as you once were. That's all that seems to matter, I guess. I'm not a scientist. I don't know the how and why of it all. We are still here, but we are also separate from it all."

Jake considered her words, then a terrible thought occurred to him.

"Am I stuck in the diner?"

"Probably not," Penny said. "Step outside and check."

Jake leapt up and ran to the door. He had no idea how to go through it, but with some focused effort, he unlocked it, threw it open, and pushed the screen aside.

One step out. Two. Three. He made it all the way to the corner of Magnetic and Main. He could smell the fresh air of the coming dawn as the branches of the ancient willow tree in the front yard swished gently in the breeze. He was clearly free to leave the diner. He turned back toward the building.

"Magnetic Ice Cream Parlor and Diner," the sign at the corner read. "You'll be drawn in every time."

Boy, that's true, Jake thought. He stepped back in the door and looked at the trio at the counter.

"So, you can go," Penny said. "Most ghosts can wander if they want. We just don't want to. We are where we are because we like it there."

Jake looked around the room. It seemed a boring place to spend too much time. Considering Penny, standing primly behind the counter, he wondered why in the world she was hanging around an old diner if she wasn't bound to it. He was grateful that he wasn't stuck inside these Coca-Cola-covered walls for all eternity.

"Well, I'm outta here," he grinned. Then, since there was certainly nothing wrong with the company of a pretty face on a grand adventure, he said, "Wanna come?" and motioned toward Penny.

Katie snorted a laugh and then covered her mouth shyly, but Penny just shook her head.

"No, Jake, I don't leave the diner."

"Are you stuck here?" he said.

"No," she answered, "I just prefer it here. Like I said."

It seemed sad for a sweet young thing like her to be all cooped up in a diner day after day. It was nice enough there for a quick meal, but why in the world would anyone stay? Certainly not him. He had miles and miles of road ahead of him and no rules or worries to hold him back. No job to report to. No boss to make happy. No rent to pay.

He couldn't see what the three of them were so upset about. This ghost thing sounded like one giant party. Jake was ready to hit the road and see what fun he could have in this new-style life. He didn't want to be rude, but they were kind of a major buzzkill, sitting there in that dark diner all mopey and sad. He took a deep breath and tried to sound calm and sincere.

"Well then, thank you, Penny," Jake said. "You've been very kind— the cheeseburger and the ice cream and all."

Penny smiled a little and nodded. She worried about sending him out into the world, but he was going to have to make his own way from now on. There was not much she could do to help him, and he couldn't stay there in her quiet little diner. He'd have to go. Jake acknowledged the other two at the counter with a brief nod, then he ventured out into the dawning day.

"Dere's gonna be trouble from dat one." Silas shook his head.

"Yes," Penny sighed. "He's bound to stir some things up, even in this ghost-ridden town."

Would she ever see him again? It was hard to imagine Jake staying contained in Eureka Springs, population 2,094-ish.

The sun was rising, and Hank and Molly would arrive soon, so Katie and Silas said goodnight to Penny and headed out the door. She locked it up tight behind them. Before the town got busy, Katie would head back to the hotel, and Silas would return to his mountain, or maybe they would just find a spot to spend the day. Maybe they'd be back that night. Maybe not. Keeping schedules wasn't a priority for ghosts facing an eternity ahead of them.

Penny cleaned the grill, washed the dishes in the large sink in the back room, and wiped the bright-red counters with a damp towel. After ensuring that everything was clean and in its proper place, exactly the way Hank and Molly had left it, she curled up in her favorite corner booth. The warm, red glow from the emergency exits was beginning to fade in the morning light. She could smell traces of Jake's burger in the air, but that should dissipate before anyone arrived, just as the vibrant energy force had dimmed once he left the building. Now there was nothing to do but wait for another day to begin.

Chapter 3

For Penny, the next few days moved along just like any others. Hank and Molly came in right after dawn and started baking and chopping, preparing tuna salads, dumplings, and cobblers for the day. The freezer was checked over and new supplies ordered. The adorable, red-topped, diner-style tables were set, and the tubs of Blue Bell Ice Cream were prepared in the display case, ready to serve the tourists and townsfolk who flocked through each day. The aroma of baking dough, sweet with apple dumpling filling or topping from the blueberry cobbler, wafted through the air.

Even if she couldn't smell it as acutely as the living, the homey odor still warmed Penny through and through. It reminded her of long-ago holidays and sitting at the kitchen table chatting while her mother prepared pies for the family. If it was a cherry pie, they would make bets on who would get the one slice that invariably had a single pit hidden in it. If it was an apple pie, her father would be called in to magically peel each apple with a paring knife in a long spiral that never broke until it finally fell away in one piece. Neither Penny nor her mother could ever do it quite like that. Penny loved to munch on the apple peel almost as much as the pies. It snapped in her teeth, releasing juicy tartness that made her taste buds tingle. One Thanksgiving, they had eaten a whole apple pie without even cutting it—just digging forks in right through the crusty center and pretend fork-sword fighting over who got the last bits of apple or tender, crimped edge.

Every single morning, the diner smelled like home and the happiest memories of family and love. For a moment, she wished that Jake were around to enjoy this experience, but she wasn't sure he would appreciate it. Alive or dead, a soul had to be quiet and at peace to benefit from the little things like the smell of baking pie crust. Otherwise, it got lost in the hustle and bustle. Jake would probably just want her to come outside into the big world with him.

Why would I want to leave all of this? Penny thought.

During the summer months, the diner was open every day for lunch and dinner. Sometimes, the couple hired a waitress or two to help them out here and there, but they preferred to take care of things themselves. In the lonelier winter months, the diner closed on Tuesdays and Wednesdays to give them some time off. The town semi-hibernated in January and February. Nobody was much interested in ice cream during the frigid Arkansas winters, but then life went back to normal by spring. Every day during the tourist season was full of cooking, cleaning, and customers.

Penny kept out of the way this morning, as she had since 1952. Obviously, she couldn't help out without reminding the couple of her constant presence or—worse yet—startling customers. Even when they were the only three in the diner, she wasn't sure how Molly and Hank would feel about having objects independently float around the room. The better part of wisdom told her to be quiet, so she stayed in her booth and waited for the customers to arrive. She'd have to move out of the way then, but that was still the best part of the day. So many different people with such interesting stories.

There were some guests who came in every week, sometimes more than once—farmers, hotel owners, shop owners, and flamboyant artists by the dozens. But in a town of roughly two thousand people, that was not the bulk of their business. Penny appreciated the familiar faces, but she adored the tourists.

People who were on vacation—on an adventure—brought an amazing energy with them. It enveloped her the minute they entered the diner. Those visitors were in the middle of exciting times outside the daily humdrum of their normal lives. Even the exhausted mothers with cranky toddlers in tow flowed with a freshness and light that they would never have on a routine Tuesday afternoon. As disheveled and disorganized as they might look on the outside, Penny could feel the radiance bursting forth from their souls.

The delicious food and fun atmosphere of the diner made tourists glow. All the Coca-Cola signs, vintage ads, ceiling fans, and wallpaper were delightful and started conversations about memories long forgotten. Busloads of senior citizens touring the city would often stop by. Seeing all of those images from their youth long ago reduced them to childlike glee. They would emanate so much joy—just from the sight of the inside of the diner and the comfort food—that Penny wished she could jump on the bus with them and keep that feeling going.

But she never did.

It wasn't like she hadn't thought about it sometimes, especially early on. And it wasn't like she couldn't go if she wanted to. After she'd first arrived at the diner as a ghost, just as Jake had a few days ago, Penny had thought she couldn't leave. It had taken her days to even try. Eventually, she'd discovered that she could open the door and walk right out. She'd even made it as far as the corner, around the bend a little, and had bravely looked up the road at Magnetic Spring and its beautiful flowers. But going farther than that was scary. No, not scary. It was downright terrifying. In the diner, her afterlife was safe, routine, and predictable, but she had no idea what might be just up the road. Normal life things couldn't touch her, she understood that much, but maybe there were other things that could.

So Penny had stayed at the diner. Year after year. Decade after decade.

In the end, after meeting lots of other ghosts as they stopped by the diner and hearing their stories, she wasn't so afraid of the outside world, but she just didn't see much point in going out into it. She read the newspaper over customers' shoulders. As the radio in the diner played over the decades, she delighted in how the music changed and rock-and-roll took over. She was amazed by the first cell phones and was captivated by watching them get smaller and smaller and fancier and fancier. She learned how to use a computer as guests started bringing in their laptops to work on during lunch breaks.

During the day, there was always plenty to observe and learn. She listened to people talk about what was new and exciting in town and what they had seen in their travels. There was no TV in the diner, but watching television had never really been a part of Penny's life before she died—television was still black and white, and there had been very few shows—so she didn't miss it.

What she had really loved was going to the picture show. Movie magic never ceased to amaze her. There was no movie theater in town, even if she was tempted to slip out in the evenings, so Penny had to count on what she had at hand. For decades she had just lived on her memories of her beloved movies.

Alone at night, she would act out her favorite scenes and try to remember the dialogue word for word. She had Gloria Swanson's crazy eyes from *Sunset Boulevard* down perfectly, always ready for her close-up, and just as easily she could become Cinderella, ready to go to the ball, imagining the mice from the diner were making her a dress in the back room. Dancing with her make-believe prince took even more imagination because she had never actually danced with a boy. What it felt like to have a handsome man gaze longingly into her eyes was harder to envision than seamstress rodents. Some nights she could have conversations with a rabbit that no one else could see, like Jimmy Stewart. Maybe Harvey had just been a ghost, she'd joke.

Then came the Internet, and Penny quickly realized that access to thousands of movies was only a click away.

At night, she turned on the computer in the office and played around, reading and watching videos. Over the quieter winter months, Penny had watched Molly or Hank kill some extra time watching videos, hidden behind the curtain in the office area. Once she learned the password and discovered how to access old movies, she would spend hours watching the ones that had been her favorites. The diner had the same Internet service that Molly and Hank had at home next door, and they clearly loved movies as much as Penny, so there were all kinds of streaming options.

Anything with Fred Astaire and Ginger Rogers was the very best. If no one came to visit in the evening, Penny would pull up one of their movies and watch it from beginning to end. She might even find herself joining in and "dancing cheek to cheek" with an obliging broom. There was something about the twinkle in Ginger's eye in that moment when whatever character she was playing realized that she was in love with whatever character Fred Astaire was playing. In just one look, Penny could tell that Ginger was thrilled and horrified and scared and hesitant and excited, all at the same time. So many emotions would flash by in just the twitch of an eyebrow.

One of her favorites was to watch Ginger's face while Fred sang "They Can't Take That Away From Me" in *Shall We Dance*. She could only imagine that *this* was what it felt like to fall in love—to realize that you were in love with someone, even if they didn't know it yet. Penny had never been in love, so she could only guess, but she hoped that was what it felt like because it looked extraordinary. She thought all of that was out of reach for her now. Dead people were past falling in love. So she just lived vicariously through Fred and Ginger, Humphrey Bogart and Lauren Bacall, Cary Grant and Deborah Kerr, and all the other star-crossed and successful movie romances from her youth.

She tried new movies sometimes, but the ones she knew from when she'd been alive were better. She wished she had still been around to see theater productions like *The Sound of Music* and *Oklahoma* on the big screen. Those grand musicals were not as much fun on the small computer monitor, but she loved the songs and the characters and the love stories. Sing-alongs were just as fun, no matter what size the screen, and the dark diner was often filled with echoes of songs that no one living could hear.

She also enjoyed surfing the Web and reading articles. There was more information out there than she could ever begin to understand, and she certainly read tons of it, but Penny enjoyed the real people who came into her home more than images on a screen. Those were the best stories.

Many troubled souls passed through the doors of Magnetic Diner. Some were still alive and poured out their troubles to Molly at the bright-red counter over a bowl of ice cream. She would listen patiently and offer bits of advice. But there were other troubled souls who were past Molly's aid.

Penny took on the job of helping the ones who had left life behind. Like Jake, some were drawn here to a comfortable and familiar spot, a spot that made them feel peaceful and happy, as they dealt with the confusion of being dead before they thought they should be. Others had never set foot in the diner before but seemed drawn there, like it was some cosmic waiting room—a moment of celestial, transitional limbo in the Ozark Mountains. Penny found that she had a great talent for helping them "go into The Light" and move on to whatever lay ahead for their now totally altered lives. It was a noble job, and Penny was proud of it. She had served hundreds of bowls of ice cream over the decades and stood by as the newly-departed vanished into the next realm of existence.

But she had failed miserably with Jake. Had the moment to move forward come too quickly for him? Should she have just blurted it all out, told him what to expect, and helped him to brace for the inevitable? It was so rare that she failed.

Knowing that Jake was still out in the world in such an unsettled state worried Penny. She had thought he might come back to visit in a day or two if he was still in town, but by the end of the week he had not returned. Maybe he had just left and returned to where he came from. Haunting a familiar place was a pretty standard ghost choice, but she had no way of knowing what he had decided once he'd left the diner.

Penny got her first hint at how Jake was doing a few weeks after his death as a random tourist spilled his story of frustration to Molly over some warm apple dumplings a la mode.

"Every morning it's gone," he fumed.

Penny had been reading an interesting article in the *Lovely County Citizen Newspaper* over a customer's shoulder, but the tone of this man's voice caught her attention. She sensed an interesting tale would follow, so she moved over and stood behind the counter—well out of the way, but close enough to hear what he had to say.

"The first morning, I may have left my keys in the ignition, I admit it, so I was just grateful when they found my bike parked in another lot up the road with the keys still there. But the second day, I know I brought the keys inside, and it was still moved. That day, they found it five miles away with the keys in it again."

"Well, that sure is odd," Molly said as she wiped down the counter near the cash register.

"But last night, I very carefully brought the keys in the hotel and put them in the drawer by the bed. How could someone have gotten to them? The hotel room door was locked. I was there all night. But come morning, my bike is nowhere to be found again. It took the cops three hours to locate it this time—all the way out at Turpentine Creek Wildlife Refuge."

"Did someone hot-wire it?" Molly asked, stopping her work in amazement.

"Nope," he said. "That's the crazy part. The keys were in it. My keys with the razorback hog on them and everything."

"Did Sherriff Jimmy have any answers for you?" Molly asked.

"Hah!" the man laughed. "Something about ghosts going for a joyride, of all the craziness."

Molly raised one eyebrow, looked around the room, and then thought the better of it. Best not to say anything, she decided. To a local, ghosts taking a joyride on a tourist's motorcycle was not as crazy as it sounded. Out of the ordinary, but not crazy.

The biker took a final bite of his dumpling, picked up the bowl, slurped down the last of the melted ice cream, and then headed for the cash register.

"Glad I'm headed out of town today," he said. "That crook is gonna have to find someone else's bike to take for a midnight spin tonight."

Molly handed the tourist his change and smiled.

"You drive safe now," she said, "and watch out for them ghosts."

The man laughed and headed out the door.

Molly had been only half-kidding. She closed the register, looked around tentatively, and then moved slowly but deliberately behind the curtain and into the kitchen area.

Penny followed her, like she always did when she felt that Molly needed her.

Molly paused in the middle of the back room. Then she took a deep breath and put her hands on her ample hips.

"Penny," she said firmly, "if you know anything about some crazy, motorcycle-stealin' ghosts, I hope you'll handle it quickly. We can't have bikers gettin' scared away, thinkin' there's thieves around here. Ghosts in haunted hotels are creepy in a funny sort of way. Tourists come to town just for that. But crazy ghosts runnin' around town makin' trouble need some tendin' to."

Molly paused another second, then nodded her head as if to say "that's all" and headed back out to the diner.

Penny sat on the stool next to the grill, her heart aching a bit. Yes, she did have a pretty good idea what in-denial, angry biker ghost might be stealing tourist motorcycles and taking them for midnight joyrides around the mountains. What to do about it was another thing altogether.

Even if Penny felt like leaving the diner, she had no idea where to begin looking for Jake. A ghost on a motorcycle might be anywhere. She could keep her ears open for any clues the customers might have about strange goings-on, but even if she got an idea about where he might be, she was pretty sure she wouldn't know how to get there. She had been just a teenager the last time she was out and about on the town. That was decades ago. How to get from here to anywhere specific was a mystery. She would just have to wait and hope Jake came back to visit her before some real trouble got started.

If the townsfolk were annoyed enough, they might call up a medium to settle things. Penny shuddered. She hoped she could spare Jake that kind of handling. She wasn't exactly sure how it all worked, but she had heard stories that made her tingle with fear.

If you were a ghost, mediums were to be avoided at all costs. Maybe that was why most of the town's ghosts stayed in places that made it their business to sell tourists on ghost stories and liked having them around. Or, like Penny, the departed kept quiet and out of the way. Being exorcised or ripped from your comfortable home by force sounded terrifying. She hoped Jake didn't keep calling so much attention to himself before she could sort it out.

Despite her best efforts to find out more, several days passed without any stolen motorcycle stories or any clues as to where Jake might be. Penny had eavesdropped on more conversations than she could count as customers enjoyed their tuna salad, burgers, and apple dumplings, but she had learned nothing. It took a visit from Silas to enlighten her.

He came by one night, moving eerily through the front door without even opening it. That always unnerved Penny a bit. She hated going through objects. It made her feel queasy.

"Silas," she murmured. "I would have unlocked the door for you."

"Ah," he chuckled, "it don't bother me none. I lives in the woods, ya know, an' I just go right through dem trees now without even noticin'."

Penny slid sadly into her favorite corner booth at the far end of the diner, stretching out her legs along the red vinyl seat next to her and leaning her back against the wall. Her ponytail made her feel that nauseating tingle as her head brushed against the Coca-Cola wallpaper, so she rested it sideways against the cushioned, red vinyl back of the booth instead. Silas pulled up a chair from the closest table and sat in it backwards so he could lean his arms across the back of the chair.

"Ya looks like ya gots somethin' on your mind, Miss Penny," he said.

"It's Jake," she admitted. "Do you remember him? The one who died in the motorcycle accident a few weeks ago."

Silas's eyes lit up.

"Oooo, dat crazy boy. How can I ferget some nutty ghost dat I sees all da time?"

"You see him?" Penny lifted her head in amazement.

"Sho' 'nough. Dere's a biker bar an' hotel just 'cross da road from my woods. He be dere all da time. I seen him come an' go."

"Is he making trouble?" she asked.

"Well . . ." Silas considered his words. "He be . . . well . . . it seem like dere be an awful lot mo' fights dan dere used ta be."

Silas scratched the short, salty hairs on his old head. He never went over to the bar himself, but big fights usually spilled out into the parking lot, so he could see and hear them from his side of the mountain. It seemed like there were two or three every night over the last couple of weeks. That added up to how long Jake the Biker had been around town. Silas could only conclude that the two probably went together like grits and corn bread.

"I think he be doin' some messin', but dey don' know it be him," he said.

"I heard Molly talking to a biker who said his motorcycle had been stolen several times and turned up miles away the next day. His keys were being stolen right out of his locked room. Molly thinks it might be a ghost. They can't prove it, but it seems pretty logical that Jake would have done it. I certainly don't know of any other ghosts in town that are so attached to motorcycles that they would feel the need to steal one. She's worried that tourists will think there is a bike thief in town and not want to come here. Can you talk to him?"

"Ooo-eee," Silas said, leaning and holding on to the back of the chair, "he be a wild one, dat Jake o' yours. Remembe' da look in his eyes? Crazy energy jus' a-bouncin' off da walls."

"Oh yes," Penny admitted, "wild to be sure. But if he's right there where you live, maybe you can let him know about the dangers of messing with the living and calling too much attention to yourself where you won't be wanted."

"Suppose so," Silas said.

"If you can come all the way off Bluebird Mountain to talk to me down in the city, you can certainly make your away across a two-lane highway to try to talk some sense into Jake."

"Yeah, but you is much mo' purdy company," he said with a wink.

Penny waved him away with a gentle swish of her hand.

"Maybe so," she laughed, "but you've been negotiating that hilltop since a little farmhouse was the only thing there almost a hundred years ago. You watched a tornado blow it all away, but they rebuilt a house double the size. You supervised that, but no one knew you were there. Families have come and gone and built a guest house and made it a tourist spot. Bluebird Restaurant across the street became a biker bar. And yet none of them along the way ever suspected you were there. You have the skill of getting along with the living down to an art. You could give seminars on it."

Silas nodded and smiled. He was pretty proud of the fact he could exist without any drama. The family living on his hill had no idea he was there. The hundreds of visitors to the guest house never noticed him. Weddings and family reunions and parties galore went on in the pavilion right in front of him, and no one ever sensed a thing was out of place. He knew how to keep quiet and out of the way. No one would ever call in a medium to deal with Silas, and he liked it that way.

He could certainly go into the bar and see what Jake was up to without calling any attention to himself. He just didn't much want to go there in such close quarters with so many people—and so much beer. He really preferred to keep his distance from all of that as much as possible. One glance at Penny's face told him that it was important to her, and he hated to let the sweet girl down.

"I'll goes by tomorra," he agreed reluctantly, "and den I'll lets ya know what's what. Maybe I can even gets him ta come see ya."

Penny frowned. Was having Jake back in her diner a good idea? Penny wasn't so sure. Remembering how it felt to be in the presence of all of that pheromone-charged electricity, Penny felt a shiver run up her spine. She didn't imagine he would cause too much trouble. Nothing she couldn't fix, at least. But he was a more animated presence than any other ghost she had run across in town, and definitely the most handsome and charming. It would be easier to have him stirring things up on Silas's mountain than in her diner. Maybe Silas could handle the misguided young biker all by himself and keep him out of her peaceful existence.

"Thank you, Silas," Penny said. Then she leaned across the booth toward him with a smile. "Would you like some ice cream?"

He smiled slyly.

"Well, ya know I do."

Chapter 4

Silas was true to his word. The next night, after the sun went down and the bikers began to gather across the street from his haunting grounds, Silas ventured over to find Jake.

Standing at the edge of two-lane country Highway 62, the road he had helped to build, Silas stared at the small blue building across the street. Neon lights in the windows offered beer from every brand imaginable. Even though he was still fifty yards away, traces of cigar and cigarette smoke wafted past him. Raucous laughter and blaring country music echoed away from the open door and down into the valley beyond. Silas ran his heavily booted foot through the gravel at the side of the road. It grated and shifted with his indecision.

In all of the decades that he had lived on this mountain, Silas had never ventured across the highway to that bar. Back when it was a restaurant, he sometimes wandered over to sit with groups of chatty locals and tourists and listen to what was new in the world, but he had not been back since the first draft beer pumps were installed. Not since it became a full-fledged bar. A place like that, full of alcohol and rowdy bikers, brought back the echoes of too many bad memories. Guilty memories. A visit would surely stir it all up again. Silas knew there was no way to fix the past. There was so much wrong done that he could never undo, not even after almost a hundred years stuck on earth as a ghost. He'd rather avoid it than think about it. He had become highly skilled in the art of avoidance.

But he would do it for Penny. She was always so kind and friendly and welcoming. On his loneliest days, he could always count on a smile and a bowl of ice cream from Penny. It was only for one night, and he would never have to do it again. Bolstered by the thought of being able to do a good deed and ease his friend's worries, Silas moved across the street toward the bar. A semi-truck blasted down the highway and right through him, but Silas didn't flinch. There was really no need to look both ways when your body was long gone.

Climbing up the steep incline from the road, Silas steeled his resolve. Even to his dimmed senses, exhaust, beer, and greasy food battled with the natural smells of the rocky roadside and made him squinch his nose. The parking lot was full, with dozens of customers milling around. It was a beautiful evening, and the warmer spring weather had brought out the adventuresome bikers in force. Some were parking their motorcycles after a long day of touring around the Ozarks and were now heading into the biker-friendly hotel rooms next door. Others just pulled right up to the bar—big "hogs" and tall-handlebarred choppers and fancy bikes with sidecars and more sedate trikes, all lined up in a row. There were dark leather jackets as far as the eye could see.

Silas hesitated outside the bar. Too many living and very high-energy people were in there. Gazing intently through the large window in the front, he could see men and women with oversized, frothy mugs and bottles of beer sitting at the bar. Some were shooting pool in the middle of the room. All of them seemed to be in jolly spirits and thoroughly enjoying themselves.

Silas shuddered. All that living, human presence made him uncomfortable. Not to mention all the beer. This was closer than he ever wanted to get, but he had promised Penny. She was always so good to him. He couldn't let her down.

Gathering all of his courage, Silas slid through the front wall of the building and tucked himself into a corner. Then he waited to see what he could see. It was half an hour before anything important to him happened, but when it did, there was no question about the fact that Jake was involved.

Silas heard the raised voices first, but then he saw a burly older man in a black leather jacket with a red bandana tied around his head leap up and grab the front of the jacket of a younger man who sat next to him.

"Ya little turd!" he hollered as he glared into the young man's startled face.

In a split second, he had punched the young man across the face and sent him sprawling violently into a table full of guests next to them. The women at the table jumped out of the way, screaming as the cold drinks sloshed onto their laps. The men sitting with them reacted by jumping on the older man and pummeling him. Men all over the room leapt into the fray, not even sure which side they were on. Silas shrank back into his corner in horror. His worst fears about coming into the bar were thrashing all around him.

Then, through the mob of brawling bikers, Silas saw Jake. He was behind the bar, nearly hidden in shadow, and he was laughing. Silas had never considered himself the sharpest tool in the shed, but it didn't take a genius to reach the conclusion that Jake had something to do with all of this chaos.

Remarkably, it was over as quickly as it had started. The bartender and other guests managed to calm the situation, and everyone returned to their seats, nursing minor bumps and bruises. But the offended younger man still wouldn't settle.

"I still say I didn't take your beer," he grumbled, grabbing an ice bag from the bartender and holding it to his cheekbone.

"Well, somebody took it!" the older man fumed back, his long, gray beard rumpled from the battle.

A white-haired woman, maybe his wife, urged the older man toward the door to avoid any further incidents, but he mumbled the whole way out. Looking back again, Silas saw Jake still sitting on a stool behind the bar, looking very pleased with himself. As Silas stared, Jake caught his eye, and his smile faded. He gazed intently at the old convict, and then stood up and moved in his direction. Silas held his ground.

"You look a little out of place here, old-timer," Jake said.

"I reckon so," Silas answered, uncomfortable to be chatting out loud with so many of the living just an arm's reach away. A ghost could never tell who might sense his presence.

"You're the guy from the diner, right?"

"Yep. But I come here a-lookin' fer ya."

"For me?" Jake asked. "What for?"

"Miss Penny be worried 'bout ya. She worried 'bout what ya up ta out here in our city. She been hearin' rumors dat sound like ya been makin' trouble."

Jake hadn't thought much about Penny since he left the diner. It was a night he'd rather not think too much about at all. Hearing that Penny was worried about him made him remember her soft smile and green eyes. He might just have to stop back in that diner again for a visit, but first he was going to have to deal with the judgmental gaze of the salty-haired old man. Silas was waiting for some kind of response.

"Just having some fun, that's all," Jake shrugged.

Silas glanced over Jake's shoulder and across the room to where the young biker now sat nursing a beer with one hand and holding the bag of ice on his face with the other.

"I don' tink dat young fella be callin' it fun."

"Oh," Jake shrugged, "it's not a big deal. These guys just get so wound up so easily. Move a few drinks around when they aren't looking, and you've got a real party started." He winked and smiled.

"An whiles dey sleepin', ya just up 'n' take a liddle ride on deir bikes."

Jake's eyes widened in surprise, but he didn't stop grinning.

"You betcha," he said. Then he thought about it twice, and his smile faded. "Does Penny know about the bikes?" He didn't like the idea of the pretty waitress being upset with him, and he doubted stealing motorcycles would impress her.

"Yes, sir," Silas nodded. "An' she ain't none too pleased. Makes da city look bad, an' makes people not wanna comes here."

Jake leaned against the wall next to Silas.

"What does she care about a city she never even sees?" he said.

"Well," Silas pondered, "I suppose it still be her city. People here comes ta da diner, an' she know 'em. Dey like her family now. When dey be sad, she be sad."

Jake considered this, but he didn't seem terribly impressed.

"There are tons of ghosts all over town," he said. "I see them all the time. This place should be used to some unexplained things."

"I suppose a few tings movin' 'round a room o' some funny noises o' doors openin' fer no reason be okay, but, well . . . tings that would land the livin' in jail, not okay."

Jake considered this. It was an interesting theory. You wouldn't think ghosts would still have rules to obey. That was annoying, to say the least. Jake had never been very big on rules and laws to begin with. Now here he was still getting lectures on them after he was dead, and from a criminal of some kind at that. It was tempting to be angry with Silas, but he seemed so old and worn-out that Jake mostly felt sorry for him. Jake could tell he was just trying to help, no matter how frustrating it all was.

Silas shifted uncomfortably, and his old work boots scraped along the rough wood floors heavily enough to make some noise. No one noticed over the blaring music. Jake looked down at his own feet, below his favorite jeans, to the fancy pair of black boots he would apparently be wearing forever. He hadn't even had them on the day he died.

Funny, what you end up wearing for eternity, he thought. *Too bad I didn't get to keep my bike.*

"I wasn't really stealing the bike," he finally said, "I only borrowed it a couple of times. I left the keys there. I just miss riding, that's all."

"Yep," Silas said, understanding exactly. He looked around the bar at all of the men and women drinking and having a good time. "I miss dis, sorta. I shouldn', but I does."

Jake looked up and followed Silas's gaze around the room, then stared back at the haggard-looking old man.

"I forgot. You were drunk the night you died, weren't you?"

Silas nodded slowly. Jake started to put the pieces together.

"Silas, did you get drunk a lot?"

Again, Silas nodded slowly.

"Is that part of why you were in jail in the first place?"

Silas's dark eyes met Jake's, and he nodded in response.

"Dem prohibition laws weren't 'round yet, not fer a whiles, an' I drank lots. All da time. I was young an' havin' fun, jus' like ya tink ya be havin' fun tanight. My folks run outta patience wif me. I stole sometime ta gets cash fer da booze. It was bad. Den it gots worse. Gots in a big fight in a bar one night, an' dere ain't no more fun o' freedom fer me. Not ferever."

"Someone got hurt?" Jake asked.

Silas nodded. He lowered his head and shuffled his feet again, tugging at the ends of the long sleeves of his prison uniform. Jake was hesitant to ask too much, but if Silas had gone to jail when he was young and died when he looked like he did now, he must have been in for a long time. Whatever he did must have been bad.

"Silas, did someone get killed?"

Silas nodded again, slowly, without lifting his head an inch.

"In da fight, he hits his head on da edge a da bar, an' dat be dat."

"It sounds like it was just an accident. Neither of you were in your right mind, and it just got out of hand."

"Maybe," Silas shrugged, "but he be white an' had a wife an' a new baby. Jury didn' take no pity. Puts me in jail fer life."

Life, and then some, Jake thought, contemplating the old ghost in his prison clothes.

"But wasn' 'nuff. Didn' make me stops bein' a drunk anyhow. Bein' drunk made it all better, an' no mo' sadness an' pain. In da jail I jus' drank when I could, ever' chance I gots on work crew, an' moonshine in da prison an' such. Drunk da night I died, but ya knows dat already." Jake nodded. "I done tried havin' a beer afer my accident, ya know, but it jus' wasn' da same. No buzz."

Jake looked back down at his feet.

"Ridin' dat motorcycle ain't da same neither, huh?" Silas wondered aloud.

Jake sighed, then he shook his head slowly.

"But I just keep trying to get that feeling back."

Silas understood that desire more than he could explain. How could he help Jake move on and face life now without the one thing he thought brought him the most joy?

"Ridin' a motorcycle like a crazy man be what got ya inta dis mess in da first place," Silas said.

"I know, I know," Jake admitted. "But I just thought that, since I can't get hurt, maybe I could ride even wilder than before. But it just doesn't feel the same. The wind isn't the same."

Silas reached out and touched Jake's shoulder.

"It tain't never gonna be da same, son," he said quietly. "No matta how many bikes ya try. We be stuck where we ain't supposed ta be. Lotsa tings is not like dey should be."

Jake nodded.

"I just get so bored," he admitted.

Silas chuckled.

"Dat'll pass," he said. "Ya get used to it. Maybe da next time dat Light come callin' fer ya, ya be itchin' to go," he joked. "Dat's supposin' ya gets anoder chance."

Jake laughed and shrugged. He had no interest in going into The Light.

"Ya should go an' see Miss Penny," Silas said. "She be mighty worried. Ya gots stuck on her watch, and she feelin' responsible fer ya."

"Okay," Jake said. He didn't need much encouragement on that front. Looking out the big window next to them, Jake scanned the parking lot, evaluating the bikes resting there.

Silas followed his gaze.

"Oh no," he stopped him. "Ya gots ta get dere on yer own."

Chapter 5

Jake did head down the mountain to see Penny, but he didn't steal a motorcycle to ride on. Silas made sure of that.

He had also made sure that Jake learned a bit about how to travel as a ghost. Walking was not required. Neither were motorcycles. Getting from one place to another was more of a thought process. Once Jake could let go and face the fact that he no longer had a material body, he got better at it. It was actually a lot like riding a motorcycle, but without the noise and vibrations. Ghosts just kind of glided along.

So Jake slid in to see Penny the next night as the diner was closing up. He waited outside, sitting idly on the flower box under the sign, until Hank and Molly locked the door and headed down the sidewalk to their house next door. Then he peeked in the window.

Penny was sitting in her corner booth with her legs stretched out along the seat. Her head was tipped sideways on the red, vinyl, cushioned headrest on the back, and her eyes were closed. Jake tapped gently on the glass to get her attention.

Penny's head snapped up at the sound, and she searched in his direction. Even across the room in the dim light, Jake could see the bright green of her eyes. He'd been a little distracted the first night they met and hadn't really noticed how truly beautiful she was, but he remembered those eyes.

Now they twinkled just for him, and she hurried over to the door to let him in, butterflies flittering around in her stomach despite her best efforts to remain calm. He was just as she remembered him—confident and handsome and full of swagger—but the energy force he brought into the diner that night was more subdued and at peace. The vibrating rage and anger from the night he got stuck had abated. Penny took that as a good sign that Jake was coming to terms with his situation and would be ready to temper his behavior, at least a bit.

For his own part, Jake had no intention of settling down and being a good dead person. Returning to the scene of the crime didn't help change his mind. The diner was the same as Jake's memory of it from that horrible night a few weeks ago. Emergency lighting only. It was eerily dark and still, even more so now with just the two of them there. Jake reached over to turn on the bank of lights near the door, but Penny immediately stopped him.

"No, Jake," she said firmly. "Never call attention to the fact that you are here if you don't know how the living will react to it."

"But why sit in the dark? They already know you're here."

"But I'm careful not to make them think about it too much. Molly likes to talk to me sometimes when she's alone, but most days they probably forget. That is how it should be. It's safer that way."

"Why in the world do ghosts need to be safe? What more can happen to me now?" Jake said.

Penny sighed. This was not going to be as easy as she had hoped. Silas might have gotten Jake here, but he clearly had not gotten him to wise up about the realities of life as a ghost. She turned around and stalked over to the counter. Her skirt flounced and her ponytail swayed with her frustration.

He's new at this. He's new at this, she reminded herself.

Sitting down firmly on a red, vinyl stool at the counter, and counting to ten in her head, she swiveled around slowly to face him.

"As a general rule, the living are terrified of ghosts," she tried to explain. "They've seen movies about horrible things happening to people who mess with ghosts or live in haunted houses. I hear the customers talk about it all the time after they've taken a ghost tour at the Crescent Hotel. It's funny to think about in an abstract kind of way. Wander through our hotel. Hear scary stories. All fun and games. But to think you are actually coming into contact with a ghost or to have one of those stories *happening to you* is a different thing altogether."

Jake came over and sat down next to her. He was trying to pay attention to what she was saying, but even in the dim light, he could see her eyes sparkling and the soft way her glossy ponytail fell over her shoulder. She looked really pretty when she was annoyed.

"Jake, are you listening to me?"

"All right, I get it, keep a low profile, yeah, yeah."

He grabbed the counter with both hands, wound up, and spun his stool around three times, arms above his head, before it came to a rest, slowly, to face Penny again. He flashed her his most charming grin. She just frowned in return. How could she make him understand?

"I knew you were going to be trouble from the moment you left here," she sighed. "Didn't you learn anything about caution from the way you died?"

"Well, what's the point of being cautious now?" he laughed. "I can't die *more*."

"Jake, you still have being. You still have existence. The energy that is your life force can't be destroyed. It just changes. Don't you understand that? We are sitting here having a conversation. You are still you. It's just different now. You and I are not where we were supposed to go when we were done with material life. There is something else. I've seen it as others move on. There is more, one way or another. Life goes on."

Jake sensed that he had a perfect opening for the big question that remained unanswered from their first visit—and a good way to change the subject too.

"So why aren't you there, Penny, in this place we were supposed to go?"

Penny sighed and shook her head.

"I'm not really sure," she admitted. "And I'm not sure why I stay here year after year. I stand right behind that counter and watch The Light come for others, but it is never for me."

"How do you know you can't go with them?"

Penny swung the stool a bit from side to side and wound her ponytail thoughtfully around her finger. She shrugged.

"I don't know how to explain it to you, but you just know. Each opportunity that comes is only for that person. The Light is focused. It has purpose and intent. I remember the pull I felt when it was my turn. It has never been the same again. So we are stuck here, and there are rules to good ghostly behavior just like there are rules to civilized living before you die."

Jake spun his stool to face the window by the front door. He felt all caged up in this dark building, being reprimanded for breaking rules. Even death didn't get him away from it. Besides, she was far too pretty to fall into the nagging-woman category in his life. Beautiful young women with sparkling eyes deserved to be up and living life to the fullest.

Jake saw his next adventure clearly. Get Penny out of this old, dated diner. She deserved to break a few rules and feel the wind in her hair, as much as a ghost could, and he was going to make proving that to her his first noble act of his afterlife—or maybe his whole life, for that matter. Just getting her to step out of the door was job one.

"Let's go outside, Penny," he said casually. "It's a beautiful night."

Penny turned and looked hesitantly through the window at the dark garden on the other side. Jake bumped her with his shoulder, a playful glint in his eye.

"Come on," he pretended to whine. "Get some fresh air."

"Fine," she agreed. "But I'm not getting on any motorcycle for a joyride to see the lions and tigers at Turpentine Creek at the far end of town."

Jake gasped and fluttered his hand dramatically around his heart like an offended southern belle.

"Why, Miss Penny," he teased as he headed for the door, "I would never be so reckless as to try to take you someplace that might bring you joy. That would be far, far too cruel." He made a mental note to get her out to Turpentine Creek to stand in a tiger cage as soon as possible.

Penny furrowed her eyebrows at him, but Jake just flashed her a charming grin.

Very funny, she thought. *He should have studied drama instead of motorcycles.*

She was pretty sure he was just changing the subject and avoiding a lecture about his behavior, but she followed him out the door and onto the front porch anyhow. He let the screen door bang behind them. Penny startled and worried that Hank or Molly might hear, but the windows next door stayed dark.

Jake started to walk down the sidewalk toward the corner, but Penny sat down on the porch step and arranged her skirt carefully. She had not been farther than the front porch in decades and did not see any point in changing that right at this moment. The moonlight streamed down through the branches of the willow tree in the front garden, and the air was serene and still. Downtown there might still be tourists bustling around, but on the outskirts of Eureka Springs, there was not a soul in sight. Not a living one, at least. Jake could walk as far as he liked. Penny knew she wasn't budging from the steps of her diner.

Realizing she wasn't following him, Jake turned back to encourage her, but then he thought the better of it and joined her on the porch step instead. He tucked in right next to her, sitting just inches away, and propped his elbows up on his knees. It was a bit close for comfort, Penny thought, but she didn't fuss about it. They were quiet for a few moments as Penny stared at the night sky she so rarely saw.

She remembered some of the constellations from science class many years ago. The Big Dipper. The Little Dipper. Orion and Ursa Major. Were any of them actually touring the sky here and now? In her little corner of the world, stars were visible to the naked eye that you could never see near the big-city lights. Those springtime stars shone and twinkled brightly down on her, whispering of faraway and unknown things. Try as she might, she couldn't figure out which stars went together to form what.

I'll have to look them up on the computer.

Jake hadn't noticed the stars at all. He stared straight ahead at the white picket fence and wondered what the story was with this pretty ghost. Why was she haunting a small-town diner? What would it take to get her to leave? She looked so content that Jake considered letting her off the hook about how she ended up stuck as a ghost, but his curiosity got the better of him. He knew why and how he had become trapped here among the living, but Penny's situation wasn't like his. She should have had plenty of time to resign herself to the fact that she was dying.

"Why didn't you go, Penny?" he asked. "It doesn't make any sense. It wasn't a surprise, like it was for me and Silas and Katie. You had to be kind of glad it was all over—being sick and in pain."

"Well, yes. I knew it was coming," she admitted. "We all did, for a couple of years. And it was pretty rough for a long time there at the end."

Penny fussed with her skirt a bit and tightened up the laces on her eternally shiny saddle shoes. She tucked a loose hair behind her ear and wrapped her arms around her knees.

"When it was finally, you know, *time* . . ." She glanced at Jake, and he nodded in understanding. "When it was time, I saw The Light as plainly as you did. I felt it too. There had been so much weakness for so long, but suddenly I felt wonderful. No pain. And I felt strong. Full of energy. I hadn't felt that way in years."

"So? Everything was great, and you felt great. Why not go with it?"

"I don't really understand what happened," Penny admitted with a shrug. "I felt all full of that wonderful Light, but then I looked at my parents. They were so sad and resolute. And I looked at my sister—my dear little sister."

"You have a sister?" Jake asked.

"Yes." Penny let out the answer with a sad sigh. "Susie. She was only five then. She looked up to me so much. I was her big sister, you know? Her whole life she had tagged along with me and done everything I did and wanted to be just like me. We didn't tell her how sick I was until those last few weeks. She thought I just had the flu or something. I kept telling her it was all going to be okay, even long after I knew that wasn't true."

Penny looked at Jake to make sure he was still paying attention, and his dark-brown eyes met hers, a bit too intently.

"It's stuff I try not to think about," she admitted, breaking the gaze. "It seems like something I should spend hours going over and over in my mind, but I haven't really thought about it since those first few days after I died. Ghosts don't talk about what happened when they got stuck. Not very often. Stuck is stuck. The 'why' of it all doesn't really matter that much."

Looking back on the worst moment of her life was not something she really wanted to do. Penny closed her eyes and could see her mother and father, with quiet steadfastness, sitting hopeless vigil at her bedside in the hospital room, as they had for weeks. They knew it was time too. The doctor had told them that she wouldn't last the day.

Thinking back, Penny wondered if maybe they had been a little relieved. The tears had been shed. Her mom was probably praying. Nothing more to be done. There couldn't be many things worse in this world than watching your child suffer, knowing there was nothing you could do to make it better. So they sat and waited for it to be over. The room reeked of antiseptic and bleach, but she could still catch small wafts of her mother's familiar perfume when the fans blew in just the right way.

Susie sat next to her, clutching her favorite stuffed rabbit, confused and sad. Her blonde curls had been perfectly brushed, and her cotton-candy-pink dress was crisply ironed, but her eyes were dark and vacant. How did you explain death to a five-year-old child? Susie had never even experienced being sick and in pain. She'd never had so much as a skinned knee. Her big sister looked tired, but how could she begin to understand sickness so bad that it takes the person you admire most in the world away from you? Penny wasn't sure if her parents had tried to prepare her. They had done it privately, if they had. Penny remembered not knowing what to say. Talking was nearly impossible by that point, anyhow, much less being eloquent about life and death and comforting to a kindergarten-age child.

There was nothing but sadness in the memory. It all seemed best left forgotten, but maybe there was an answer for her if she looked back. *Why am I stuck?* Penny sighed and opened her eyes. Jake nodded encouragingly.

"Go on," he urged. "What do you remember?"

"Well," she continued, "The Light came for me, just like it did for you and all those others I've seen in the diner over the years. But I knew this Light was for me. It was peaceful and wonderful, and I could feel it pull at my very soul. In that moment, while I was all full of The Light, I was still conscious of my family in the room. Tears were pouring down Susie's cheeks, and I could see she was clutching my hand, even though I couldn't feel it anymore." She hesitated, remembering that surreal moment.

"Like this?" Jake took Penny's hand and clasped it firmly between his own.

She gasped, startled at the unexpected contact. It was like an electric jolt through her body. No one had touched her, not really touched her on purpose, in more years than she could remember. Maybe not even since that final desperate grasp of her sister's hope to keep her alive. Certainly, in her short earthly life, no wildly handsome young man had ever held her hand. Penny's eyes met Jake's, wide with surprise, but he just smiled and nodded, still holding on firmly.

"What happened next?" Jake encouraged.

Penny regained her composure and tried to recall that night again. Pulled back into the memory, Penny frowned at the thought of it.

"It was a really long time ago, but I remember feeling sorry for Susie. I must have stopped breathing or something because she knew I was dying. Her little face was so panicked and terrified. I was worried that she would feel lost and lonely without me. That she would have trouble coping. It broke my heart to think of her being left all alone."

Penny was quiet a moment, staring at a jagged crack in the sidewalk. Then she lifted her head as a very specific memory hit her.

"She begged me not to go," she whispered in awe.

"What?"

"I'd forgotten about that. Susie was crying and clutching my hand, tears all over her sweet little face, and she begged me not to go. She said she couldn't live without me. Then The Light was gone, and I found myself standing in the middle of the diner. We had been here dozens of times while we were in town, so I knew *where* I was. It just took me a while to figure out *why*."

"Magnetic Diner," Jake sighed, nodding toward the sign a few feet away. He read the words inscribed there. "You'll be drawn in every time."

"I suppose so," she shrugged.

Suddenly keenly aware that he was still holding her hand, Penny pulled away gently, tucking her hands deep into the folds of her billowy skirt. Jake let her go, but he stayed close.

Then after a minute of quiet she asked, "Was that it? Did she want me to stay so much that The Light went away?"

Jake shook his head.

"I don't think so," he said. "If that were true, spirits would be stuck around everywhere. Most everyone who dies has someone wishing they wouldn't. No, it sounds to me like you didn't want to let her down, so you didn't go. But your body was done, and you had to live a different way."

"I chose not to go?" Penny said, amazed.

"My nana would say, 'The spirit is willing, but the flesh is weak.'"

Jake smiled sadly, thinking that his nana would be proud he could quote at least one bit of Scripture. She had certainly tried to pound enough of it into him to change his wild ways—not that it had helped at all. Penny glanced at him curiously, trying to absorb the irony of Biblical wisdom coming from somewhere inside his rebellious mind.

"Not wanting to go is not the same thing as really being able to stay," he went on, determined to continue to impress her. "You know, some people are caregivers, Penny. They worry more about everyone else than they do about themselves. Mind you, I don't know a lot of those people in real life, but I've heard about it, you know, on Oprah and such."

"Oprah?" Penny said with a laugh. Jake grinned.

"They used to have her show on every day in the lobby at the bike shop where I worked."

Penny smiled, trying to imagine Jake imbibing life wisdom from Oprah, his face streaked with motorcycle grease. He was an enigma, that was for sure. This softer side of his personality, quoting Oprah and the Bible, was easier to handle than his raging, testosterone-filled persona. She wrapped her arms around her legs, pulling her knees up tight, and stared up at the stars.

"And what life wisdom did you learn from Oprah?" she asked. "I can't imagine her advising folks not to worry about each other."

"No, but she always had really stern words for those people who are so giving that they end up not taking good care of themselves too. She'd do stuff like send them on a special vacation."

I take care of myself, don't I? she wondered.

Jake pondered Penny's years in the diner, helping other newly deceased folks find their way into the Light, but putting her own life on hold.

"I bet she'd send you on a very long, very special vacation," he said.

Penny smiled at him, but she couldn't imagine any vacation spot that would pull her away from this town and her beloved diner. She had never been much of a wanderer in her short life. Home was always the best place to be, and that hadn't changed one bit in her afterlife.

"Why do you stay here?" he asked. "You said you can leave, but you don't."

"Where would I go?" she said. "Here it is peaceful, and I have Silas and Katie and some other friends who come around now and then. I watch movies and read at night. During the day, hundreds of interesting people come and go. And lots of people like you show up— the newly dead and extremely confused—and I help them along. Life is good here."

"But how long has that been going on? You say that life doesn't ever stop, but it looks to me like your life sure has. How can you possibly be content with a couple of friends and a tiny diner in the middle of nowhere? You comfort Silas and Katie. You wait around to help others make that transition into The Light. But what about you?"

Jake touched her face gently and turned it to meet his. That same tingling sensation rippled from her cheek down her neck.

"Sometimes, Penny, it gets to be about what *you* need and want."

She hesitated as his dark eyes focused on her, eyes full of worry and concern. No one ever worried about Penny, and it was certainly the last thing she had expected to come from Jake. Wasn't she the one trying to help him with the afterlife? The sensation was unnerving. Leaning back, she shook free and turned away from him.

"What difference does it make?" she said. "I'm dead, and this is what there is now. I just try to make the best of it and do a little good where I can."

"Is 'the best of it' sitting around a diner for over, how long is it now, sixty years?"

"I don't know," she shrugged, rising and walking over to the white picket fence and leaning against it. "This feels like where I am supposed to be. It's home now."

"You can go anywhere and do pretty much anything you want," he said, "and you don't have to worry about getting hurt or worrying anyone."

"Silas and Katie would worry. Hank and Molly would worry," Penny said. "They would notice I was gone and worry about me." But even as she said it, she was not so sure.

"How would they know you left? Molly and Hank, I mean," Jake said in frustration. "How do they even know you're here at all?"

"That's kind of a long story."

"Where do I have to rush off to?" he said, stretching out his legs in a dramatic show of getting comfortable, crossing one booted foot over the other and leaning back on his elbows.

Penny hung onto the fence, swinging a little bit at the end of her outstretched arm. Her skirt swished softly back and forth. Then she let go and walked over to an outdoor table a few feet away, sitting on one of the bright-red ceramic chairs with a Coca-Cola emblem on the seat. The outdoor seating area and surrounding garden were really beautiful. Rock walls with carefully tended flowers ran around the outskirts and enveloped Penny in the love and care that Molly and Hank put into the diner.

I need to come out here more, she thought. *I could even help Molly with the weeding without upsetting anyone.*

Her relationship with Molly was an odd one, to be sure, but it made her feel special and needed and important. She hadn't talked about it for many years, but Jake was settled in, and there truly wasn't anywhere else to go, so she started at the beginning.

Chapter 6

"I'm not really sure how Molly knew I was there the first time," Penny admitted.

"Can she see you?" Jake asked, intrigued.

"No," Penny said, "but something happened and she could *feel* me, I guess you could say. She could sense that I was there."

"So . . . what happened?"

This was more actual talking than Penny had done in ages. Usually friends stopped by and chatted to her while she listened and nodded. No one asked her much of anything—not a ghost or a living person. Ever. It was disconcerting to have someone—not to mention such a charming and intense someone—asking her difficult questions and truly expecting answers. Jake waited patiently to hear the story, his legs still stretched out casually down the steps, so she tried to put it into words.

"I had been here for about forty years, I guess. It had been a long time, and no one had ever noticed me before. There have been some other owners of the diner since 1952, you know. When I first arrived, there was a family with six kids running the place. I loved watching them do homework in the corner booth and having ice cream after school. Back then, the diner was pretty much the same, but they were just starting to collect all of the Coca-Cola stuff. And things that are quaint now were actually in style. Once their kids were grown, they sold the place and moved to Florida to retire and never make another hamburger again. That's what the wife said to her friends at their going-away party." Penny smiled, trying to remember what she had looked like.

"Hank and Molly both waited tables here while they were in high school, back in the early '70s. Then Hank took over as manager, and they got married right after graduation. They bought the diner when those owners wanted to retire a few years later. What were their names? It's been so long I don't even remember. Anyhow, I had been around a long time—and I had been a part of Molly and Hank's lives for maybe twenty years—before Molly discovered me.

"Lots of ghosts used to pass through the diner then, just like now. About once a week, during the night, someone would just appear, usually near the counter area, like they were lost. Just like you."

She looked cautiously at Jake, not wanting to upset him. He shrugged and nodded slightly.

"I had gotten really good at comforting them and helping them to move on into The Light to whatever came next. During the day, I stayed out of the way. I had learned how to use things, to be able to move material stuff, so I could serve those troubled souls some ice cream. But I'd also been really careful to put everything back exactly the way it was so no one would notice. I didn't want to worry Molly and Hank about seeing stuff moved around.

"Then one day, after all of the customers had gone, Molly just slumped down at the counter and started to cry. It was like she'd been holding it in all day. That was really shocking because the two of them never talked about anything but work when they were here, and they left as soon as the place was clean. Not that night.

"Hank came right over to her, but when he tried to hug her, it just made it worse. She sobbed and sobbed and said she was sorry, but he didn't seem angry at her. He mostly seemed sad too. He said it would be okay, and they would get past it."

"Get past what?" Jake asked.

"I didn't know. Everything with the diner seemed to be going fine. Nothing was different at all. But then Hank started talking about how wonderful their life was and how well the business was doing, so I knew it wasn't about that. It was unlikely that Molly had done something terrible to him. They were such a good team and treated each other so kindly, but she just kept sobbing and saying she was sorry.

"This went on for what felt like forever. It was horrible. She just cried and cried and wouldn't be comforted, and there was certainly nothing I could do to help. Such a dear, sweet woman, who always listened to everyone else's problems and helped them feel better, and there was nothing I could do for her.

"Finally, she had cried herself out. She told Hank to go on over to the house. They live right over there, you know . . ." Penny waved a hand at the small white house next door, "and that she wanted to be alone for a while. I could tell he didn't want to go, but after she shooed him off again, he finally left."

"So, did you make her a bowl of ice cream?" Jake joked.

Penny looked at him with a little half-smile, then down at her lap.

"No," he laughed. "No, you didn't."

"Okay," she admitted, "not at first. I just felt so sorry for her and wanted to help, so I sat down next to her, kind of the way I did with you when you arrived. I just wanted to reach out and hug her. It was frustrating to have that gulf between us. But then, she looked up and right at me."

"But you said she couldn't see you."

"She couldn't. Not with her eyes. But I guess with me that close and feeling so worried about her, she could feel something there. She reached out and touched the air, which meant that she was reaching right through me. It's an odd sensation. Has anyone done that to you yet?"

"No," Jake shuddered, "and I'll pass on finding out how it feels."

"Well, I'd never had it happen to me so directly either. I mean, some people had accidentally passed through my arm or something if I wasn't paying attention. But Molly's touch that night had such need and such intent and direction to it that it . . . well, I *felt* it. It scared the lights out of me. I fell over backwards, and the stool I had been sitting on started spinning around."

"Oops," Jake smiled.

"Yeah, big oops," Penny said. "I'm very careful about not moving anything while people are around. I was just so startled. But the funny thing was that Molly didn't jump up or run or scream or anything. She has lived in this town her whole life. People here talk about ghosts like they are stray cats and dogs living in their homes and businesses. Maybe that's why it didn't scare her. She just stared at the spinning stool and then looked around a bit, like she was trying to find me.

"She said 'Hello?' hoping I would answer. I have never had anyone hear me, and Molly was no different. I answered, but she didn't flinch. She shook her head. Maybe she thought she was just imagining things. It made me really sad to think that she was so upset and now she thought she was imagining crazy stuff. So I did the one thing I knew I could do."

"You got her some ice cream," he said.

"I got her some ice cream," she nodded. "And not just any ice cream. I knew her favorite was the Blue Bell Mint Chocolate Chip. I'd heard her tell customers that for years. So I went over to the case, opened the glass door, lifted the lid on the tub, used one of the clean scoops and a fresh bowl from the stack on top of the case, and dolloped out two big spoonfuls. I tucked a spoon in the side and set it on the counter in front of her."

Penny stopped, remembering the stunned look on Molly's face. In hindsight, maybe floating bowls and ghostly ice cream serving had not been the best way to calm her nerves.

"What did she do?" Jake asked.

"For a couple of minutes, she just stared at the bowl on the counter in front of her. She didn't say anything. She just stared. Then she got up hesitantly, walked over to the door, turned out the lights, and left, locking up behind her. She didn't look around for me. She just made straight for that door. After she left, I cleaned everything up as carefully as ever and waited for morning."

"That can't be the end of it."

"No, hardly," Penny laughed. "When she and Hank arrived in the morning, Molly was edgy. She probably hadn't slept very well. But more than that, she kept looking around the room warily. The first thing she checked was the counter where she had left the ice cream. Well, that was gone now. Everything was washed and put back in place. Then she checked the tub of ice cream. It wasn't a new tub, so it was hard to tell the difference between what scoops I had made and what was served during the day. It didn't really clear anything up for her.

"There was a lot to be done to get ready for the day, so she got on with it. I was pretty sure she hadn't said anything to Hank because he didn't seem put off at all. He just set the tables and got things ready without any fuss, but Molly was quiet and tentative all day. Once all the customers left, it became clear why. She was figuring out what to say to me.

"When all the cleanup was done, Molly told Hank to go on home while she wrote the specials for the next day on the chalkboard. You know, the one that hangs up on the wall behind the counter?"

"With the big Coca-Cola bottle cap on top," Jake finished.

"Well, of course," Penny laughed. "She erased the whole board, which was weird because normally she just changes a couple of items. Then she went around the front of the counter and sat back in the same stool she had been on the night before.

"I wasn't quite sure what to do next. She just sat there, but I knew something had to be up with the chalkboard. Then she started to cry again. Not big sobs like the night before, just gentle tears rolling down her cheeks. I moved over to where she was, but this time I went behind the counter so she couldn't bump me like she did before. But when I moved near, Molly looked up and around, as if she could sense me but not quite locate me. She moved her hand through the air around her and said, 'Hello? I know someone is there.'

"Well, it took all of the courage I could muster, but I reached out and put my hand on top of hers. It doesn't feel uncomfortable when you do it on purpose. I wasn't sure if she would actually feel it, but she flinched a little, so I could tell she felt something. Then the tears really started to come. I moved away because I thought I'd upset her more, but she reached out for me, so I put my hand back. She said that, since I could move things, maybe I could write on the chalkboard. I'd never really thought about it, but I guessed I could too. She asked me to write my name.

"It had been decades since I'd written anything, but it seemed like a way I could communicate with her. So I went to the board and tried to pick up the chalk. It wasn't any different than a spoon or a bowl, and writing was like scooping the ice cream. It used the same kind of pressure. So across the top of the board I wrote 'PENNY.' It wasn't very pretty, but it was legible."

"Did that totally freak her out?" Jake asked.

"Her eyes got really big, but I think she was actually expecting me to be able to do it, so she wasn't scared. We were both quiet for a few minutes, then I thought about something I really wanted to know. I wrote 'Why sad?' on the chalkboard.

"Molly wiped a tear away, as if she had forgotten they were there. I thought I had pushed this strange communication too far, gotten too personal, or just upset her again, but she remained calm. She said that she and Hank had been trying to have a family for many, many years, and they had just found out that it was never going to happen. Something was wrong in her body, and she would never have children.

"That was just the saddest thing I had heard in a long time," Penny said. "For someone so full of love and care to not be able to have a family was completely unfair. After a few minutes I wrote 'Adopt?' on the board. Molly explained that she and Hank were pretty old now, and they didn't have much extra money for all the legal fees and costs that can go with adopting. She didn't think they would be able to adopt and maybe that was just the way it was supposed to be for them. No children. Ever."

"Maybe that's the truth," Jake suggested.

"I suppose," Penny said, "but it was still terribly sad. I lived here when the owners had a flock of busy, joyful children. Their mother's eyes would light up every day when they burst in the door from school. Those children were her whole world. Her energy would change when she even talked about them to customers. There's just nothing on this earth like having a family, and dear Molly was facing eternity without one. I was about to go around the counter and sit next to her, when she asked another question. She wanted to know how old I am. I had to think about that one. I mean, I was seventeen when I died, but that was a long time ago. I wasn't sure how to answer. Molly sensed my hesitation, and she rephrased her question. She asked how old I was when I passed on.

"That was more specific, so I wrote '17' on the board. Molly smiled. That seemed to make her happy, somehow. Maybe she thought she had been communicating with some wrinkly old lady. The fact that I was only a teenager when I died made her happy. I hadn't realized how tense the energy was in the room, but I felt it change and ease. She shifted in her chair a bit, wiped away the rest of the tears, then she said, 'I'd really like a bowl of that ice cream now, Penny, if you wouldn't mind.'"

Jake threw back his head in a big, hearty laugh.

"So did you get her the ice cream?" he asked.

"Of course," Penny smiled, smoothing her skirt in embarrassment, but then laughing too.

"Ice cream meets all the needs of the living and the dead," Jake laughed.

"You'd be surprised," Penny smiled.

"And do you still write messages with her on the board?" he asked.

"We did it once or twice more, over a few months, but then she just got comfortable with knowing I was there. I sat with her one other time, when her mother died, but that was it. Sometimes she talks to me after everyone has gone, but mostly it seems like she's just talking to herself. When she told me what you had been up to with the motorcycles and asked me to help make it stop, that was the first time she had addressed me so directly in years. She must have told Hank about me at some point not too long after that first encounter, but he never tried to communicate with me. He says 'hi' and 'bye' sometimes, but that's it. I think I make him a bit uncomfortable."

"So why stay?" Jake said. "It doesn't sound like they'd really notice if you left. Don't you want to get out and use the time you still have here on earth to have some fun and see things you never got to see when you were alive?"

Penny stood up and moved back over to the fence. Holding on with both hands and leaning way back, she gazed up into the swaying branches of the huge willow tree that stood majestically in the middle of the front yard. It had been here even longer than she had, and it appeared to be content. Then again, the willow tree had roots in the ground. It had no choice but to stay put. She leaned a bit over the fence and down into the wide drainage ravine below. A translucent layer of water flowed gently over the rocky bottom, heading for the White River or somewhere else close by. The water wasn't sticking around, but that was its job. It had a mission to be elsewhere, and that ravine was designed to move it along on its way, no matter how deep it got. Penny let go with one hand, swung around, and leaned on the fence, facing Jake.

"I can't leave Molly," she admitted. "I think ever since that night I have known that, just by being around, I make her feel better. She likes talking to me when she's sad, kind of like that daughter she never got to have. There's nothing wrong with that, is there?"

"I suppose not," Jake said, "except that it's pretty one-sided. She gets to feel better, but you are stuck day after day after day in the same old boring place."

"Boring?" Penny said. "No, it's not boring. Okay, maybe in the winter a little bit, but that doesn't last long. Lots of people come and go, and I love to hear their stories. I'm not bored."

"But you're not really living either," Jake added.

Penny shrugged. "No, I'm not living. I'm dead, Jake, remember?"

Jake sighed and shook his head. He got up and walked over to stand next to her at the fence.

"You know what I mean," he said. "It's not the same as what everyone thinks dead is. You still have life, and you should be living it. You may be able to leave this diner, but you are acting like you're stuck here in this place where you are only half of what you could be."

"The Light has never come for me again," Penny said flatly. "I've seen it come for so many others, but I always knew it wasn't for me." She hesitated for a moment, then admitted, "And I guess I have also been kind of scared to try to go. Who knows what's out there? I know what to expect every day around here."

"I have a feeling there are no motorcycles at the end of that Light," Jake joked, "so I have no intention of going toward it if it comes for me again."

"Oh, Jake," Penny laughed. "Maybe there are more motorcycles than you could ever dream of."

Jake pondered that for a moment, a heaven filled with Harleys, then smiled. Penny's eyes were sparkling again with the same vision of a cloudy field of motorcycles, ready for the taking.

Damn, she's pretty when she lets her guard down.

"You want to know a secret?" he said, leaning close enough that their bodies almost touched. Nothing about being dead kept him from noticing that she was just the perfect height to rest her head on his shoulder and tuck in nicely under his arm.

Penny gazed up at him, eyes wide, but she nodded slightly.

Leaning in closer and barely brushing her ear with his lips, he whispered, "I can dream of all kinds of things."

Penny jumped at the tingle that touch sent through her neck and shoulders, and a wild surge of electricity flowed through the air around them. He was certainly a force to be reckoned with, but the ridiculousness of ghostly flirting was too much. She just shook her head and playfully shoved him away. If ghosts could blush, Penny's cheeks would have expressed her feelings freely.

"I'm sure you can," she laughed, "but dreaming something doesn't ever make it real. I've watched hundreds of people move on, but I still have absolutely no idea what's waiting for them in that Light."

They leaned on the fence for a moment and imagined their own visions of what might be waiting on the other side of that transition.

"Maybe we are not stuck," Penny said. "Maybe we just haven't been ready to go yet."

"Maybe," Jake answered. He knew he wasn't. He wasn't ready to leave everything he knew on earth, and now he certainly wasn't ready to leave Penny. A bit of charming female company had definitely been missing from his life over the last few weeks. Most of the ghosts in town were old, and the pretty, young townsfolk and tourists couldn't see him. Penny could see him, and she could clearly feel him as well.

Watching her profile as she stared up into the night sky, Jake could suddenly imagine better uses of his time in the moonlight with a pretty girl than all of this talking. Casually stretching his arm out along the fence behind her, Jake leaned in closer to Penny again. Her eyes widened, but she did not pull away. It was hard to see her expression clearly in the dim light from the porch lamp, but Jake felt encouraged by the fact she didn't move.

Does kissing feel the same as a ghost? he wondered.

Penny hardly knew how to react, and she had no frame of reference to compare kissing before and after death, but it was a moment she had watched in movie after movie. It was the pose the leading man hit right before he leaned in for the kiss. It was certainly not a scene she had imagined for herself over the years—standing toe to toe under the willow tree with a handsome biker. Half of her wanted to run her fingers through his wild, dark hair. The other half wanted to tidy it up and focus on the fact that she was supposed to be teaching him how to behave as a ghost.

You know he's nothing but trouble, she reminded herself, *even with all of that Bible and Oprah talk,* but Jake's magnetic presence defied reason.

Every fiber of her being trembled as Jake reached up and tucked a loose strand of her hair behind her ear, letting his fingers drag gently across her cheek. His other hand pressed against the small of her back, drawing her closer and sending electric tingles up her spine. Their eyes held for a long moment before Penny closed hers, preparing for the inevitable kiss that she longed for and dreaded at the same time.

But their moment was broken by a voice from inside the diner.

"Hello?" the stranger called out. "Is anyone there?"

Chapter 7

They both stood, staring into each other's eyes, stunned, but then Penny pulled away frantically and ran for the diner. Jake beat her there, launching up the porch steps in one bound and throwing open the screen door. Inside, sitting at the counter, was a very bewildered-looking, crinkly old man in red flannel pajamas and matching slippers.

"Are you open?" he asked.

Penny let out a horrified gasp and then checked herself. A shocked reaction from her was not what this man needed right now. Regaining her poise, she walked over to him, slowly and calmly. Jake just stood holding the door, not sure what to do.

"It's a little late," she said in her best waitress voice, "but I'd be happy to help you."

"I'm not really sure how I got back here," the man said.

"Back here?"

"Yeah. I had lunch here today with my church group. We came in on a tour bus to see *The Passion Play*. I thought we'd all gone to bed, but now I'm here."

"That happens sometimes," Penny said, being sure to keep her conversation casual and comforting. "Would you like some ice cream?"

"A little late at night for that much dairy," he said.

Then he got an odd, faraway look in his eyes. He gazed longingly over her shoulder. Penny didn't have to turn around to know what he saw. So many times. Year after year. The radiance of The Light filled the diner.

"Ooohhhh," the man exclaimed. He smiled with the glee of a young child who had found exactly what he wanted under the Christmas tree. Then he was gone.

"Holy crap!" Jake yelled from the doorway.

Penny just smiled and relaxed.

"Well, that was easy."

"That happens all the time?" Jake said, still in shock.

"Yep."

Penny sat down at the counter and daintily spun her stool around, just once.

"Did you see his face?" Jake asked in awe.

"Yep. I always do. That's the best part."

"It was good, whatever he saw. It was really good. He looked . . . excited."

"They usually do."

Then she paused and spun her stool to look at him directly.

"What did you see, Jake, when that Light came for you?"

Jake let the screen door close gently behind him. Instead of coming over to the counter, he sat down at a table near the door, like he was staying close for a quick getaway. Penny could tell he was thinking about her question because his dark eyebrows were furrowed. He shifted uncomfortably.

"I don't think I really saw anything specific," he finally admitted. "It was more of a feeling. A pulling. I've seen lots of movies and TV shows about people 'going into The Light' when they die. I thought that if I didn't go, I wouldn't die."

"It didn't quite work out that way."

"No." Jake shook his head. "Dead anyhow."

He shuffled his feet under the table for a minute. Then he got up the courage to ask.

"Penny, what did my face look like?"

She frowned. There was no nice way to answer that one.

"You said you always watch their faces," he continued. "I remember you looked so calm and happy in that moment when The Light came for me. Then you didn't. I could tell you were really angry."

"Not *angry*," she assured him. "It had been a really long time since I'd seen someone refuse to go. It's only ever happened to me a few times in all of these years. I wasn't angry at you for staying. I was shocked, mostly. Then I just felt sad for you."

"Sad?"

"Being stuck is not what was planned for you, Jake."

"You think there's a plan?"

"Yes, I really do."

"You mean like heaven or something like that?"

"I don't know. Probably not the whole Renaissance-artistic thing with angels and harps and puffy clouds, but it is good. When they sit here at the counter—when they see what is ahead—there is so much joy and peace and happiness on their faces. No one is ever scared. They just look full of childlike glee."

"I didn't look that way," he guessed.

"But I think what you said explains part of that, Jake," she continued. "You said you didn't see anything. You didn't really look. You were so angry that you didn't give it a chance. You made a conscious choice not to go."

He considered that for a moment.

"Promise me something, Jake," she said seriously, so intently that he gave her his full attention.

"What?" He shuffled a bit under her focused stare.

"Promise me that if you feel that pull again, see that Light, all of that, that you will at least look. Pay attention and look at what you are being offered."

"I promise," he agreed.

She watched his face, waiting to see if he laughed or made a joke out of it. He had agreed awfully casually and quickly.

"Really," he assured her. "I don't promise to go, but I'll pay attention. It was just so jarring the first time."

"I know."

"Penny." He sat up straight and folded his hands sternly on the table in front of him. "You have to promise me the same thing."

Penny swayed her stool back and forth.

"Penny?" he insisted.

"But they need me here," she started.

"Do you mean to tell me that you think being stuck was 'the plan' for you? That you are supposed to spend decades in this diner watching other people live and love and have lives?"

She shrugged and spun the stool around once more.

"What did *you* see, Penny?" he asked quietly. She paused and faced him again. "What did you see all those years ago when The Light came for you? Was it scary?"

"No," she admitted. "I mean, I don't think so. I didn't really look either. I was so focused on my sister and my parents that I didn't pay any attention to The Light. I felt the pull, the draw of it, but I didn't really look. Then it was gone, and I was here, and that was that."

"And you haven't felt that even once since then?"

"No, not once."

"But you think the chance comes again for the people who are stuck?"

"Yes, sometimes," she admitted. "I've never seen it happen, but ghosts like Katie who spend time with lots of other ghosts in the hotels and shops around town tell stories about it happening. She's told me about ghosts who have been around for decades, and then, one day, they are suddenly gone. No one really knows how or why it happens, but it does."

"So it could happen again for you, even after all these years?" he asked.

"Yes, I suppose so."

"And you promise to pay attention and give it a chance if that next time comes?"

"Okay," she nodded slightly, "I promise to give it a chance."

Jake thought Penny looked awfully pretty when she was lying.

Chapter 8

After their night of almost-kisses and halfhearted promises, Jake started coming to visit more and more often. Whether it was just Penny in the diner, or even if others had come to call as well, he would have grand tales to tell of some trick he had played on a tourist on the street or some other random mischief he had caused in town. Penny was right. Jake was trouble. Mostly it was innocent stuff that was nothing more than annoying. No more stealing motorcycles, but he was still highly enjoying his afterlife and causing great dismay for the unsuspecting living who crossed his path.

"I wish I still had my cell phone," he joked one night. "I could make some serious prank calls."

"Oh, Jake," Penny laughed, "they wouldn't be able to hear you. And besides, you couldn't use anything that required the warmth of a human touch for the screen." She had learned this by trying to use a Kindle book reader that was left in the lost and found one day. A ghostly touch just didn't work.

"I should set up a Facebook page and 'friend' everyone I knew. That would give 'em somethin' to talk about."

Penny didn't mention the fact that there was a computer in the diner's office. Jake might be teasing, but he might really try to do it. She had never seen a ghost so interested in interacting with the living. He was clinging to that old sense of life and what was important then far more than was good for him.

It wasn't like Penny hadn't used the computer to look anyone up. The Internet provided an unending stream of information about everyone. One long winter night she had managed to find her childhood friend Nicole, who used to live next door. Her nickname was Nicky, and Penny's father used to joke that the two girls were as close as the spare change in the bowl on the kitchen counter. Penny and Nickle, he would call them. They were constant partners in the minor crimes of youth—like running wild on a summer afternoon when they were supposed to be reading in ladylike fashion or practicing piano.

It had been hard to find her. Her family had moved away before Penny got sick, and they had lost touch quickly. Preteen girls were not great letter writers. Nicole had gotten married and changed her name, but she had kept her maiden name as her middle name, so Penny was finally able to discover her online profile and see that she'd turned out just fine. That was many years ago now, but her friend had looked very much the same if you covered up everything but her eyes. People's eyes don't alter like the rest of them does. Penny was glad to know that her beloved Nickle was safe and happy and healthy, but there was no point in anything beyond that. The dead can't interact with the living anymore. Not really. So what was the point of freaking out your friends? She just didn't understand.

Jake was making an art form out of annoying the living. He still enjoyed switching around drinks at the local bars and causing a scuffle now and then. He had also discovered Basin Park in the heart of downtown Eureka Springs, and he regaled Penny with stories of flipping baseball caps off teenagers' heads and messing with the sound system during music events so it would make random squealing noises. Tapping tourists on the shoulder seemed to be his favorite game.

Katie, Silas, and any other ghosts hanging around would laugh at Jake's antics, and Penny would join in to be a good sport, but most of the time, she just didn't get it. She was too worried about the people Jake was taking advantage of to find humor in their confusion, but his endlessly charming smile kept her from scolding him. She didn't want to sound motherly. Not to Jake. So she smiled, laughed when others laughed, and served them all ice cream.

As much of a troublemaker as he was, Penny began to look forward to his visits and waited expectantly for him to arrive and stare into her eyes and give her the attention she had not felt for decades. When Jake showed up at the diner, Penny had to fight the desire to giggle nervously when he wasn't saying anything funny and hide the fact that her palms would get sweaty. Could a ghost get sweaty palms? Apparently so, or maybe it was all just in her mind. The days flew by faster with the prospect that Jake might come to visit at night.

He was handsome and charming and daring and delightful, and he brought a vibrant energy into the diner that no one else ever had. In her quiet, alone time, Penny would ponder that moment under the willow tree when he'd slid his arm close to her and up along her back. She was positive he had been about to kiss her if they had not been interrupted.

What a scoundrel, she thought.

Even fully aware of his recalcitrant nature, Penny was sure she would have let him kiss her as many times as he pleased. It felt silly after all these years to be obsessed with kissing and flirting and boy stuff, but no young man had ever tried to kiss her in real life. Not at only fifteen, before she got sick. Not in 1950. Times were so different then. Back then, no respectable boy would have dared. Now just thinking about the possibility made her feel only seventeen again, like not a year had passed.

The nights Jake didn't visit, Penny wondered where he was and what he was up to. She would put on one of her favorite movies, but one ear was always listening for his arrival. She felt a bit ridiculous to be waiting for a young man to come calling, but she couldn't help it. Was he gazing into someone else's eyes or just playing pranks? Probably a bit of both, she usually concluded. It wasn't a comforting answer.

In reality, there wasn't any other ghost in town to call on that interested Jake, but he often got caught up in his pranks and spent the night elsewhere. Just because a group of bachelorettes couldn't see him didn't mean he couldn't enjoy their party in his own way. Being a ghost was rather like having access to the video camera on every computer in town and a hidden camera in every hotel room. Jake could slip in and out of wherever he chose to be, and no one was the wiser. He was the ultimate fly on the wall, buzzing wherever he chose.

Of course, Jake never shared the seriously bad behavior with Penny. In all of his recent visits to the diner, Jake hadn't tried to kiss Penny again, but he flirted like an expert. He made her the center of attention, flattered her, told her stories of the outside world to make her laugh, and gazed deep into her pretty eyes. There was no rush. Jake was confident Penny could be convinced to leave the diner eventually. He knew the right time for making a move would present itself, and Jake had a long-term plan. Old-fashioned girls like Penny needed to be wooed, and history had proven that he was very skillful at wooing. Jake wasn't sure exactly why making her happy and getting her out of the diner had become so important to him. Maybe it was because there wasn't much else to worry about. Maybe it was just, as his TV idol Barney Stinson would say: "Challenge accepted."

Penny was caught between appreciating Jake's efforts and being highly aware of what he was up to, at least as far as the seduction went. It left her with an internal battle of logic versus desire when he was present and after he left. She was suspicious and flattered and hesitant and sometimes downright annoyed—all at the same time—but she had discovered that being with Jake was better than being without him. After decades of basically being alone, it was a disconcerting sensation.

Late one night, when it was clear Jake would be absent, Penny tried to distract herself with some Jane Austen. She had to laugh at a scene in the movie of *Mansfield Park,* where Fanny and her sister Susie talked about the debonair and downright naughty suitor who wouldn't take no for an answer. When Susie inquired about his character, Fanny was hesitant. She admitted that she was pretty sure he was "a rake"—very naughty, with a terrible reputation and a tendency to break hearts. With a rebellious gleam in her eye, Susie said she thought a man like that sounded delightful, but Fanny assured her that rakes were more amusing in books than in real life. This did nothing to dampen Susie's excitement. A thrilling rascal was still a thrilling rascal, and being pursued by one sounded like a grand time.

Penny heartily agreed. Jake amused a great deal in real life, and there was a definite thrill to being the object of his attention. Penny could imagine having that same conversation with her own sister, Susie, if they had been allowed to grow up together to become young women and share secrets about boys and love. What advice would Susie have given her then? Enjoy the ride or snap out of it? Jake, her naughty suitor. Jake the Rake. It had a nice ring to it. He might well take great pride in such a title.

As if to prove his rakish and incorrigible side, Jake would even stop by during the day and tap on a window to get Penny's attention. He would wave and encourage her to come outside. She would just shake her head and shoo him away. He was a hooligan and she knew it, but his attentions made her feel all flittery. It was ridiculously illogical.

Unfortunately, those window taps attracted more attention than just hers and often made customers turn and look. Of course, none of them could see him. Molly could hear the taps too, and not being able to find the source made her fidgety. Penny would notice her frowning and staring at the window. The presence of one quiet ghost was okay, but more than one was a bit eerie. Penny didn't like to see her friend upset, but what was one to do about a ghost like Jake?

Katie, the maid, came back to visit one evening, just as the diner was closing for the night. Penny had not seen her for a week or two. Being away for so long was not unusual, but Katie seemed to have an urgent purpose in coming tonight. She didn't bother to bring anyone from the Crescent Hotel with her, and she tapped her foot anxiously as she stood on the corner, waiting for the living to clear out. As soon as Molly and Hank left, Katie moved through the wall and sat right down at the counter, folded her hands in front of her, and looked Penny straight in the eye.

"So, I suppose you've heard about what that rascal has been up to."

"You must mean Jake," Penny sighed.

"Well, who else would I be meanin'?" Katie sassed back. "I know he's been paying you some extra attention, comin' 'round all the time with his pretty smile and puppy-dog eyes. So I had to be sure you knew all about what he's been doin' while he was on his own."

"Oh, Katie. You've heard plenty of his stories, just like I have."

"Yes, but he only tells ya what he wants ya to know. I hear things. I don't say much because I think it's good for ya to get the giggles a bit, but I couldn't let this one go. It's just too far."

"What now?" Penny wondered. Even as charming as Jake was with her in private, deep in her heart she worried about that rebellious part of him that had driven a motorcycle off the side of a mountain and stolen them once he was dead. She was pretty sure he didn't tell her about everything he was up to. No matter how much she stressed the rules of his new life, he was not one to be easily tamed.

"Every day I hear about some mischief he's pulled in town. Taking a cell phone from one pocket and putting it into another. Spilling drinks in bars. Even blowing up a skirt or two."

That last one shocked Penny. *Blowing up women's skirts in public?* But the worst was yet to come. Penny sat down next to her and nodded her head.

"Go on," she sighed.

"Well," Katie began, totally exasperated, "in the dining room tonight at the hotel, I heard two fancy ladies talking about what happened to them while they were shopping in town. They were in that store up on the hill that sells all the itty bitty ladies', you know . . ." she looked around like someone might hear them, "*foundation wear,*" she whispered.

Penny nodded. Katie was quite fascinated with the lacy offerings at The Fine Art of Romance and had mentioned it often. Katie smoothed out her skirt, as if the mention of underwear required some recovery of dignity. Tucking loose wisps of curly, auburn hair behind her ears, she composed herself and began again.

"Anyhow, the ladies were trying some things on in the dressing room, so you can only imagine what a state they were in, when suddenly the changing room curtains flew open! One lady said it was like a huge wind just blew through the store."

Penny groaned and put her head in her arms on the counter.

"The poor salesgirls were able to close it all back up and restore order, but you can imagine that those rich ladies were traumatized. Flashing their goodies to everyone!"

Penny propped her head up on her hands dismally.

"And you think Jake was in on this?"

Katie scowled at her.

"Of course I do. And so do you."

Their conversation was interrupted by Jake's entrance, walking right through the front door without even opening it.

He has certainly gotten comfortable being a ghost, Penny thought.

"Saints preserve us, here's the devil himself," Katie said.

Jake looked startled by such a strange greeting and none too pleased to see Katie at the counter. This early in the evening, Penny was normally alone, and he could have her all to himself.

"You must be full of stories today, saucy lad," Katie said, as she spun her stool to face Jake. He and Katie had crossed paths a few times around town, as well as at the diner. She normally seemed quite amused by his stories, but he only shared what he thought those present would find funny. He spared them what would earn him a lecture. Jake had no need for bothersome, judgmental women in his afterlife.

Penny smiled at him weakly.

"I hear you had quite a day," she said.

Jake looked confused for a moment, but then he realized that Katie was a true town know-it-all and had surely brought some gossip with her tonight. He had been very careful about which of his antics he shared with Penny. Just enough to seem exciting, but not enough to come off like a creeper. He kept those adventures to himself. He slowly pulled out a chair at a nearby table and sat down to take the brunt of their scolding.

"What would your mother think of how you are spending your afterlife, Mr. Thatcher? Just a bunch of tomfoolery and nonsense," Katie said.

Jake shrugged.

"I've no idea what she'd think. She ran off when I was three."

That thought made Penny sad, but it certainly explained a few things. Some good old-fashioned mothering would have done Jake a world of good.

"What about your pa then?" Katie went on.

That was the funniest thing Jake had heard in a long time. He slapped his leg and threw his head back with bellows of laughter. It was almost a minute before he could stop laughing long enough to answer. Katie glowered, and Penny shifted uncomfortably, waiting for Jake to let them in on what was so hilarious.

"My dad?" Jake gasped. "He'd crack open a beer, smack me on the back, and be prouder than a peacock."

That explained a few more things, but Katie looked more frustrated than Penny had ever seen her. Penny contemplated bringing Jake's nana into the conversation. If she'd made him memorize Scripture, she must have had some kind of sway on him, but Katie was on a roll not to be interrupted.

"Why don't ya just get yerself off to some big city where ya can do all those crazy shenanigans and no one'll care?" she fumed.

Jake just grinned.

"I've been thinking the same thing myself," he admitted.

Penny raised an eyebrow. Her one hope for Jake had been to be a good influence on him, and she certainly had grown to enjoy his unveiled efforts to charm and court her. The thought of him leaving made her stomach flip and settle heavily around her knees. A world with no more Jake at all would be a depressing place. In the back of her mind, she had always known it would happen. She knew he'd get bored around here, especially when winter came and there were no more tourists to mess with, but she was devastated to know his escape was imminent.

"Jake," Penny said, "think about that some before you run off."

"I have thought about it," he said, sauntering over to stand close to her at the counter—on the far side from Katie, "and you should come with me."

That idea made Katie throw up her arms in disgust. Penny was just shocked.

"Go with you? You mean away from town completely?"

"Sure," he said, wrapping an arm around her waist and leaning in close. "It's time you got out of here and did some living."

She just sighed and rested her hands on his chest. Jake had overestimated his charm on this front. All that rebellious, undisciplined energy was back again, flowing freely through the diner and bouncing around, mixed up with the agitation that Katie was venting.

Was this what Jake had been hoping for with all of his late-night visits and private whispers and subtle touches? Had he lost his mind completely? She didn't much like venturing out into the garden or sitting on the front porch, much less just taking off into who knows what. *Do some living?* What kind of living did he have in mind? Chaos and disorder and causing trouble from one end of the earth to the other? She tried to respond calmly and temper the frantic energy in the room.

"I'm doing just fine right where I am. I keep telling you that. And anyhow, what you call *doing some living* is a waste of spirit. We are not living anymore, Jake, not really. It's all different now. There's no point in some grand adventure. Why can't you understand that?"

"Because I *feel* like I'm still living." He let her loose and began pacing the floor. "It's different, but I still have all the energy and desires and need for something to do that I ever had. This small town is driving me crazy!"

Penny suddenly began to worry about what he might do in such an agitated state. Desperate to keep him from leaving just yet, she led him over to the counter, back again a seat or two down from the still fuming Katie, and gently put her hands over his. Her peaceful energy flowing into his calmed him down some. How to make him understand that she couldn't leave with him was another matter. It had never even occurred to her. The thought of being out and about in the wide world terrified her to her core.

"Jake," she said quietly, "I can't go with you."

"But why not?" he half whined. This might not have been how he envisioned the whole thing going down, but he couldn't wait much longer. All of that time and energy spent trying to gain her trust had been for nothing if he was going to have to leave without her.

"You just have to accept how things are now," she said. "This diner is my home. It's where I belong."

He shook his head.

"We're young and free and have the whole world ahead of us," he insisted.

Katie and Penny both smiled. They locked eyes, and Katie nodded at her. It could be the missing piece that would help Jake understand.

"Oh, Jake," Penny sighed, "*you* are young."

Jake looked from Katie to Penny, eyebrows furrowed in confusion.

"You both look young to me," he said.

"I was young when I died, that's true, and I look young to you, but I have been hanging around this diner since 1952. Years still pass, and we continue to grow up and change and mature." Penny did some quick math in her head. "I guess that would make me almost eighty or so."

Jake pulled his hand away at the thought. He looked at Penny and could see from the calm smile on her face that she was totally serious.

"Heaven help me, I'd be over a hundred," Katie laughed.

"Okay, that's just weird," Jake cringed.

"I know," Penny said, "but that's how it is. You have all of that youthful energy to go out and grab life, but we've been stuck here on earth a long time, and that feeling has long since dimmed. Frankly, I'm not sure I ever had that kind of wild ambition. I need stability and comfort and peace. Even when I was alive, before I was sick and knew my options were limited, all I ever wanted was that proverbial house with the white picket fence and a small family to love and care for. Maybe a sweet cat to sit with me while I read in the afternoon," she smiled. "I never felt that need to jump up and grab life by the horns like you do."

Jake pondered this concept, but Katie suddenly appeared not so humored by it. She grasped her hands down in her lap and stared at them, like she had the night Jake arrived. A jagged sigh made her whole body heave.

"What's wrong, Katie?" Penny asked.

"I don't know," she said. "I just realized that I'd be more like a hundred and thirty years old. Merciful heavens. I guess things here just go on the same from day to day. You know, time doesn't really feel the same. I hadn't thought about how long it has been. How much I missed out on."

Penny smiled weakly and shifted over to lean closer to her. Reaching out, she grasped Katie's hands. Penny hadn't really put a number on it before then either. It was disheartening to think she'd gradually become an old lady just sitting in her diner. How could so much time have slipped away?

A tear rolled down Katie's cheek and surprised them both. Tentatively wiping her face with her free hand, Katie decided to face the losses that ghosts learned to avoid thinking about.

"We had big plans when we got to America," Katie finally said. "It was the turn of the century, and everything was exciting and new. Pa and Ma were gonna get some land out West. We'd have a little farm and wouldn't need to ask anybody for anythin' ever again. I had a fella too," she sniffed. "We were gonna get married and have a whole flock of wee ones."

"But then you died," Jake said.

But Katie shook her head.

"No, then all of them died."

Jake and Penny exchanged surprised looks and then waited patiently, hoping she would explain.

"We had made it to Independence, Missouri," she said, "to join up with the other folks headin' out on the Oregon Trail. It was dangerous, we knew that, but if we could make it to the end, all our hopes and dreams would come true."

"Did they die on the trail?" Penny asked.

"No, we never even made it out of camp. One morning, everybody got really sick. Ma, Pa, and my twinkle-eyed Ryan, they were all dead by bedtime."

"Cholera?" Penny asked. She remembered learning about that in school. It was a terrible disease that got into the water, especially along the Oregon Trail, and killed whole families in a few hours.

Katie nodded.

"I think so. That's what the doctor said, anyhow, but he didn't want to stick around and really check into it. We were just a bunch of immigrants, and he didn't want much to do with us, especially once everybody was dead. I was sick too, but not as bad as them. Some kind church folks scooped me up with the little bit of belongings I had and brought me here. They hoped the magical healing waters in the area would help. They had heard the legends of the Sioux Indian chief, whose daughter's eyes were healed by the Eureka Springs water, and all of the settlers who swore by its healing power."

"And it helped, I guess," Jake said.

"Maybe," she shrugged, "and maybe I just got better. They were nice folks, but I wanted to be on my own, to take care of myself. I was pretty enough and smart enough to get a job at a nice hotel, so as soon as I was able, I did. Bein' a maid was about the only respectable line of work for an uneducated Irish lass my age in those days."

"What made you think about all of this today?" Penny asked.

"Don't know," she admitted. "I guess hearin' Jake talk about still wantin' the same things. That's true enough, I suppose. You don't stop wantin' what you wanted before. It just gets lost in the monotony of life, day after day."

The three of them were silent for a few minutes.

"I guess," Katie finally said, "I guess I wish I'd gone that night when I fell down the stairs. That's what was supposed to happen. I wasn't supposed to be stuck here with nobody to love me for over a century."

Penny grabbed her friend and embraced her, enveloping her in an energy force full of caring and concern.

"You know you can always come here," she whispered in her ear. "I love you, Katie. I'm your family now."

Katie pulled away hesitantly and wiped her eyes again.

"I know, Penny, you've been a good friend, but it's not enough. It just feels like there's somewhere else I'm supposed to be." Katie's voice trailed off, and a strange look came over her face. It was almost like . . .

Penny felt a vibrant electricity engulf the room, ten times more powerful than what had been coming from Jake and Katie. The hairs on Penny's arms and the back of her neck tingled as the diner filled with a brilliant Light. Katie's whole face began to glow, and a radiant smile spread from ear to ear, but she was no longer looking at Penny. Her gaze rested over Penny's shoulder at The Light that was just for her.

"Oh," Katie gasped. "Hi ya."

And then she was gone.

"Wooo hooo!" Jake yelled, slamming his fists on the counter. "That was awesome!"

Penny sat frozen in shocked silence.

"Did you feel it?" he said. "The energy? It's like a bolt of lightning came straight up out of the floor!"

Jake swam his arms around in the air in front of him, spinning on his stool and relishing the remnants of tingling electricity.

Penny nodded slowly. It had felt different than others that she had witnessed. But then again, she'd never actually seen someone get a second chance.

The stories are true. The Light does come again.

"Who do you suppose she saw?" Jake asked.

Penny's mind drifted in a startled fog. She was still tingling all over, like Katie had passed right through her.

"What do you mean *who*?" she asked absentmindedly.

"She said 'Hi ya' to someone. Didn't you hear her? She saw someone in The Light. From the look on her face, I'd say it was someone familiar."

Penny tried to clear her thoughts. Was there someone special waiting in that Light for Katie?

"Maybe it was her fiancé," Jake pondered, "or one of her parents. Did she have any brothers or sisters?"

Penny just shook her head.

"You know as much about her pre-ghost life as I do," she admitted. "She never wanted to talk about it. Most ghosts don't."

Jake considered this for a moment.

"But look what happened when she did talk about it," he concluded.

Penny weighed that observation and found it interesting. Katie wanting to shut out those thoughts of love and family that were part of her past life might have been what kept The Light from coming back. Penny and Jake locked eyes.

"Anything you want to talk about?" he asked.

Penny shook her head quickly. That thought was terrifying. Who knew what might happen with all that post-Katie energy still buzzing around the room. What would Molly do if Penny was suddenly gone? What kind of trouble would Jake get into? Who would help the lost souls who came through the diner every month? Logically, she knew The Light wasn't something to be afraid of, but it was still daunting.

"What about you?" she asked him.

"Not a chance," he smiled. "I don't think it would have the same effect on me, anyhow. Not much warm and fuzzy I'm going to remember about my life."

That was depressing. Except for the pain of being sick, which she really couldn't remember anymore, her life had been filled with loving, caring family and friends.

"Let's get outta here," Jake said, jumping up and heading for the door. "I need fresh air and open sky. It's too dark and quiet in here."

Penny half wanted to go, to be where he was, but somehow big, open sky sounded more scary than refreshing. She felt comfortable in her diner. Being there was safe.

"Not tonight," she said casually. "I've had enough excitement, thank you."

Jake grinned.

"Never enough excitement for me," he said.

"But you won't leave town yet?" she asked hopefully.

"Not just yet. I'll give you some more time to think about it. Hasta la vista, Miss Penny," he said, giving her a brief bow, and then he whooshed right through the door with a flourish.

The town better watch out tonight, Penny thought.

Chapter 9

Left alone in the dark diner, Penny worried about what trouble Jake would get into after he left. He was something else, that was for sure. When she was alive, he wouldn't have been allowed within a mile of her nice, proper life. Her mother would have shaken her head in despair and refused to let her out of the house if Jake had come around.

"You are not stepping out with that hoodlum, Miss Penelope," she would have said, "and that's the end of that."

The notion made Penny smile. She didn't often think about her mother or her father or her happy world from when she was young and healthy and alive. It made her ponder on Katie and her sudden departure when she was willing to reminisce about the happiness and love in her life.

What happened to make her ready to go so quickly after over one hundred years? Was it just the thinking about it? she wondered.

Penny had told Jake the story of her death and the love surrounding it, but The Light hadn't shown up for her. None of it made any sense. But that wasn't the biggest of her worries. Jake was going to leave, and soon. She certainly hadn't been looking for a man in her life, but now that it seemed she had one, Penny couldn't imagine his permanent absence. But could she leave with him? It was unthinkable. Live without him around? Illogically depressing. Why in the world should she miss such a maddening presence in her life just because he flirted with her?

Penny had never been one of those boy-crazy girls, and she highly resented finding herself slipping into that role at this point in her life. It was ludicrous. Of course she wouldn't run off with crazy-man Jake, but being certain of that didn't help her feel any more at peace about it.

It was one of those nights she wished she could slip off into the emptiness of sleep. Instead, she pulled up *Swing Time* on the computer in the office and lost her thoughts in a world of Fred and Ginger, where everything was simple and every love story had a happy ending.

But the real world came right back at her with the daylight. Without his magnetic personality right at hand, she had managed to come to terms with Jake's removal from her life. What niggled at her now were thoughts of Katie. She hadn't ever really categorized it that way, but Katie was the closest friend she'd had since she died. It was nothing like the unquestioning, youthful best-friend-forever relationship she had experienced with Nicole. Nickle. If they had gone to high school together and worried about things like dances and boys and marriage, certainly their friendship would have changed too. It might have become more like what Penny and Katie shared.

For decades, she and the Irish maid had sat in the diner together in the wee hours of the night and chatted about nothing of any importance. They had shared ice cream, and Katie had kept her up-to-date on what was happening around town and at the hotel. Wasn't that what friends did? Yes, Katie had been her friend. Her flaky, frivolous, gossipy friend. Now she was gone forever.

But even more than worries about missing her companionship, Penny kept revisiting the look on Katie's face before she vanished. She just couldn't shake the image of it. What was it that her friend had seen in that Light? Was it the love of her life, Ryan, or maybe her parents? Was it something even more?

Molly and Hank arrived, and Penny watched them prepare for the day as she had thousands of times before, but her thoughts were elsewhere. She was so distracted that she was startled by guests sitting down at her favorite corner booth—with her still in it. She had to climb over the back of the seat to avoid making contact. Brushing up against the living was not the way to start out any day. She tried to clear her head and listen to the tourists' conversations, but her mind kept drifting to Katie and Jake and how so much of what was peaceful and secure in her life had been suddenly and irreversibly upended.

Focusing on the music on the radio often helped when she was having a bad day, but today it just made things worse. Penny had never really thought about how many songs about heaven there were until they all echoed through the diner on the same day. Sitting on a stool in the corner, Penny could not escape them. First came an old '80s song. "Heaven isn't too far away," Warrant crooned. Next, Johnny Cash warbled "Meet Me In Heaven."

Lines in that song about walking into a light across the bar and how they would still recognize each other when they met again beyond the stars made her think of her friend Katie. Was she somewhere in that Light now? What was she doing this morning? Was there a diner on the other side of whatever change came with letting The Light take you? Were she and Ryan sharing ice cream there and catching up on a hundred years of time spent apart?

Bryan Adams sang about "Heaven." Eric Clapton mourned for his son with "Tears in Heaven." *Is everyone else hearing this?* No one seemed to notice. She also couldn't miss that all of these songs talked about love and heaven in the same breath.

Belinda Carlisle assured her that in heaven, love comes first, as she sang about the heavenly touch of her lover right here on earth.

Love. Penny thought longingly about the way Jake would stare into her eyes, the way his arm felt around her waist, how giddy and weak-kneed and like a silly schoolgirl she became when he stood closer than he should. Was he in love with her? Was she in love with him? Or was it more just the thrill of something different? Her parents had loved her and so had her sister, but it was not the same kind of love. Penny had never felt romantic love in her lifetime, that love that she enjoyed so much in movies, so she didn't have anything to compare it to. Could a man annoy you so significantly and still be your one true love? Deep within, she hoped not. She hoped she had more self-control than to be in love with the likes of Jake, but was love that controlled and simple?

Then the radio played a new jazzy song she normally enjoyed: "Locked Out of Heaven." The lyrics were a little dicey, but she'd gotten used to that over the years. Penny watched some teenagers dancing in their chairs to the beat. They waved their arms in the air and sang the refrain loudly, greeted by smiles from others in the diner, but all Penny could think was, *Am I locked out of heaven?* Was she shut out from feeling whatever was behind that look in Katie's eyes right before she vanished—the look all of them had before they went into The Light?

But it was hard to be mopey and introspective with all of the frantic activity buzzing around her. Things in her diner today were at a fever pitch.

It was the July Fourth weekend, and everyone who came through the diner was in an especially vibrant mood. Even the locals had festivity in their souls. There was talk of the parade in the morning and fireworks out at Holiday Island the next night. Every chance she got, Molly ran back into the kitchen to work on prepping special trays of food for parties all over town.

Molly and Hank loved the Fourth of July. In one day, they would make as much money as in a whole month of normal business. There were catering jobs for parties around town. There were ice creams and cold sodas and hamburgers to be served after the parade. What was a holiday for everyone else was their biggest day of the year. Everything seemed to move at double time. Penny just tried to stay out of the way. She could avoid the people, but she couldn't get away from the frenzied atmosphere.

She never went outside during the day, but by the afternoon, Penny had endured enough songs about heaven and happy people and laughter and fun. None of it included her. It had been decades since she had been so keenly aware of the limbo she lived in. Today, she felt so frustrated that she wanted to scream. For the first time ever, her delightful diner felt oppressive and lonely. She had ventured as far as the garden just a few weeks ago. Maybe it would offer a reprieve.

Moving carefully through the room to avoid any contact with the living, who would surely be full of overwhelming energy today, Penny waited for her chance and slipped out before the screen door swung shut. It caught the back of her heel as she took her last step. *Eesh.* She hated that feeling. It wasn't painful, like it would be to someone alive, but it didn't feel right.

Her hopes of some peaceful outdoor space were quickly squashed. There were only more people and decked out cars and American flags everywhere. The diner was on the Independence Day parade route, so all along the natural rock walls across the street there were decorations galore. Small flags on wooden sticks were jammed into every crack and crevice.

Squinting against the sun, Penny noticed a familiar face, a ghost she rarely saw, sitting on a rock outcropping across the way. It looked a bit quieter over there, so Penny took a deep breath, looked both ways to avoid having a car pass through her, and headed boldly across Main Street.

"Well, look at you, all brazen and sassy, just waltzing your way across the main drag," the waiting ghost said.

Penny giggled, let her breath go in a puff, and sat down on the rock.

Penny had not seen Donna in years. In her past life, Donna had been a local and a regular at the diner, but as a ghost, she didn't come to visit. Not since the night four years ago when she had arrived at the diner in the middle of the night—and gotten stuck, like the rest of them. It was incomprehensible to her that a massive heart attack should take her away at only sixty years old, and she had no intention of going anywhere.

Donna had driven a trolley tour around the town her whole adult life, and the thought of leaving her dear little community was too much for her. Penny found it interesting that Donna's ghostly attire was one of her more lacy and frilly "period costumes"—the kind she always wore to help put folks in the mood for their tour of the historic downtown area. Her dark hair was in a neat bun at the base of her neck, and her head was crowned by a large-brimmed, white lacy hat. She looked ready for a stroll down Mud Street in 1880.

Penny had heard that—in her afterlife—Donna just rode around on the trolleys all day and fussed about what a poor job the new drivers did. She gave her own personal tour and included all of the highlights that the newer guides missed. Of course, no one could hear her.

Maybe I should be like Jake and take a trolley out at night and host all of the local ghosts for a city tour. That idea lightened Penny's mood considerably.

"Well, you're all smiles now," Donna said. "When I saw you come outside, you looked like a tourist stole your ice cream."

That image made Penny smile even more.

"No," she laughed. "All of my ice cream is accounted for."

"Then what's going on with the famous ghost guider at Magnetic and Main?" Donna asked.

"Ghost guider?"

"Well, sure," Donna said. "Everyone in town knows what you can do. Folks who are on the verge of being stuck just slide on away when they are faced with those pretty green eyes."

"I don't think that has anything to do with it," she said meekly.

Donna laughed.

"Well, maybe not, but you sure do somethin' right."

"I didn't help you to move along."

"Oh, honey, there wasn't a power on this earth that could have convinced me to move on. A spirit hellbent on staying is not going to be swayed by some Rocky Road and a pretty face."

It was comforting that Donna didn't blame her for being a ghost. Penny always felt guilty, even as rare as it was, when a soul that should leave into The Light got stuck. At least she knew now that it wasn't a permanent situation. She had proof of second chances at whatever lay Beyond. Penny thought again of Katie, and she looked down at her eternally shiny, black-and-white saddle shoes, swinging idly off the edge of the rock.

"Did you know Katie, the maid from the Crescent Hotel?" she asked.

"I've seen her around," Donna said. "Kind of a gossipy little thing."

Penny shrugged.

"She left last night."

"What, left town?" Donna asked, surprised.

"No." Penny made a sweeping motion up into the air with her hand. "Left. Whoosh. Vanished. Went into The Light."

"Wow!" Donna leaned back against the rock wall behind her. "The infamous second chance. You saw it?"

Penny nodded solemnly.

"You made it happen?" Donna asked, wide-eyed.

Penny shrugged again.

"Not intentionally. No, I don't think it was me. She just got to remembering about her family and her fiancé and all the things she had missed out on. It really hit her that she'd been stuck for over a century. She said that she wished she had gone the night she fell down the stairs and died. The night she was supposed to go."

"Thinking about those things opened the door, so to speak? Wanting to go made it possible for another chance to come?"

"I guess so," Penny admitted. "It kinda makes sense, you know?"

Donna nodded.

"Have you tried it?" she finally asked.

Penny shook her head. *No, NO, NO!* she thought, but she answered more calmly.

"That's pretty terrifying."

"Why? Don't you think it's about time you moved on?"

Penny smiled at that concern, coming from another ghost who had no intention of going anywhere anytime soon.

"You chose to stay here and no one fusses about it," she said.

"Yes," Donna admitted, "but I'm out and about and living how I want to every single day. I have made a choice, for right now at least, to stay here. You watched me make it that night I refused to go."

Penny had to acknowledge the truth of that. She had sat right at the counter with Donna the night she consciously became a ghost to haunt her beloved town. It wasn't quite the same as being stuck.

"You are not just stuck, Penny," Donna continued, as if she could read her thoughts. "You're in a rut. Same old, same old, day after day. That's not life. Oh, honey, your soul may as well be buried six feet under with your body."

Penny shrugged and swung her feet. Up until the last few weeks, she would have challenged Donna and insisted that life was wonderful and amazing and exciting in her little diner. Now, she was not so sure.

"You know what they say," Donna began, "the only difference between a rut and a grave is the depth."

Penny half-smiled but then she considered what that meant for her life.

Am I in such a deep rut that I've made it a grave? she thought. *Am I more than just stuck, like so many others?*

Penny gazed across the street at the diner. Her diner. Through the big front window she could see Molly joking with a customer and Hank scooping up a huge, pink lump of ice cream into a cone for a tiny little girl.

"I like it here," she admitted. "It would seem odd to leave and go into whatever is in The Light."

Of course, going into The Light wasn't her only option for leaving the diner. Jake had made a blunt invitation. Donna had lived a good, long life. Maybe she would have some motherly advice to offer.

"Have you run across our new club member, Jake Thatcher?" Penny asked her, trying to sound nonchalant.

"Oh, heavens, yes," Donna laughed. "That's a wild and wooly one, for sure. What's that song say? I knew he was trouble when he walked in. Mercy. He's gonna be stuck for a while, but I don't imagine he will stay around this small town much more."

"No, he plans on heading out soon. He even wants me to go with him."

Penny glanced at her shoes. Donna noticed her look and smiled.

"Oh, so it's like that, is it?" she laughed. "Has Miss Green Eyes got a crush on Mr. Rebel Without a Cause?"

The thought tickled Donna to no end. She threw back her head and hooted a big guffaw that normally would have made everyone turn and stare. Of course, no one around but Penny could hear her.

"Maybe, it seems kind of like it," Penny smiled. "Crush is a good word for it. He's charming and handsome and all that, and it's great to have someone paying so much attention to me. It feels good, I admit it, but I don't see how it would work. I tried to explain to him that I'm really an old lady in my soul, but I don't think he believed it."

"Well, folks see what they wanna see and believe what they wanna believe on both sides of the grave," Donna said, still chuckling to herself.

Penny nodded. So true.

"Well, he believes I'm young, like him, and that we should run off and have a second life together."

"Oooh," Donna sucked through her teeth, "and what does our little Penny think about that?"

"I told him no," she smiled. "There's not much that's tempting about the reality of dashing around the countryside with a crazy young boy. Even when I was a teenager, that wasn't my style."

"From what I hear, you never got to be a real teenager, Penny," Donna said, suddenly serious.

Penny considered this. She had found out she was sick when she was fifteen. She died when she was seventeen. Not exactly super-fun, rebellious years.

"I suppose not," she admitted.

"And now?"

Penny reconsidered it, trying to imagine an afterlife with Jake the Rake. Would he love and care for her? Could they haunt some little house with a white picket fence together? How many weeks would it be before he would become bored with her and abandoned her for new adventures? How many days or even minutes? There were bound to be other pretty, young-looking or actually young ghosts all over the place, if one had an eye for them. Then where would she be?

A little part of her niggled inside that it could be fun to get out and go. A life with Jake would certainly be full of adventure and new sights and experiences. Did it really need to be about love? The unfinished teenager in her heart longed to be young and free and desperately in love with the charismatic bad boy. The mature woman deep in her soul whispered that he was a heartbreaker, and she would regret upending her peaceful existence for him. If she truly believed that Jake loved her or she loved him, should there be so many what-ifs?

"I bet it would be a hell of a good time," Donna said with a grin.

"Maybe, but no," she said. "Still no." When it really came down to it, Penny knew that she would miss Molly and Hank, her diner, and this town more if she left it all than she would miss Jake if she stayed behind. She would miss him, but not enough. That wasn't how a woman was supposed to feel about a man she loved, and it did matter. At least to Penny. Love was what she needed. A Fred and Ginger kind of love. A Bogart and Bacall kind of love. A love that filled up the heart and soul and being and finally made everything feel complete and whole. That earthly desire hadn't ebbed at all in the years that she had been stuck in this half-existence between life and what lay beyond. She had squashed those feelings down deep inside because it no longer seemed possible, but Jake's magnetic presence had brought it all bursting forth again. Penny wanted love, and Jake was not capable of providing it.

Donna watched Penny's face as she pondered her feelings for Jake. Then she smiled and said, "'There could have been no two hearts so open, no tastes so similar, no feelings so in unison, no countenances so beloved.'"

"What?" Penny asked in confusion at such a strange statement.

"It's from Jane Austen's book *Persuasion*. It's how she describes the true love between Anne and Captain Wentworth. I spend a lot of time in the library now," Donna admitted.

"Oh."

"And I was just thinking of those beautiful words and wondering if that is how you feel about your Jake."

Similar tastes and feelings. Hearts in unison. Penny certainly wanted someone she could open her heart to and trust that their feelings would be in unison. No, it was not Jake.

"He certainly has a very pleasing countenance at least, as Austen would say," Donna teased.

Yes, very pleasing, but that wasn't enough for the future that she dreamed of. Penny found herself startled to even be thinking of what lay ahead. For decades, she had just moved on from day to day without expecting anything to change. She wasn't sure if she should be grateful to Jake for making her think beyond tomorrow or if she should be angry that he had rumpled up her comfortable existence. Jake was certainly not "the one," she understood that now, but he had awakened the hope in her heart that finding a soulmate was not a thing of the past. Even now, Penny yearned for that more than she had realized. She sighed at the very thought of a kindred heart. Was he out there somewhere? Maybe he was still alive. Maybe he was already in The Light.

"Should be quite a parade tomorrow," Donna observed, tacitly changing the subject.

"It always is," Penny agreed.

The two of them sat on the jagged, Ozark limestone rock ledge, legs swinging, and observed the celebrating crowds going by. Little girls leapt around in fancy red, white, and blue dresses with half a store's worth of ribbons in their hair. Classic cars cruised by with enormous, patriotic paper mums tied to the front grills. There were pickup trucks full of teenagers, mostly sunburnt and crispy from a day on Beaver Lake, ready for parties on that steaming summer evening. The little girl with the giant, pink ice cream cone came out of the diner and followed her family across the street, where they enjoyed their treats on the front lawn of the funny little fake house that showcased all the delightful architectural styles of the historic district. Trolley stop #73, just a few feet from where Penny and Donna sat, picked up and dropped off tourists, filling the diner with a new flow of frivolity and celebration.

It was delightful to be here, watching it all pass by as she had since 1952, but Penny wondered if there was something even bigger and more wonderful waiting for her. Something that had nothing to do with Jake or her diner or Eureka Springs.

Amid all the excitement, Penny couldn't help seeing in her mind's eye the joyful look on Katie's face before she'd left. Something was there that Penny couldn't quite put her finger on because it didn't all make sense. There was only one word she could apply to the feeling exuding from Katie before she wafted through Penny's being and vanished: relief.

Chapter 10

"I'm staying for the parties, but that's it," Jake announced near dawn as he blew through the front wall full force.

He'd been thoroughly enjoying crashing the parties around town all night and was in a stellar mood. Coming back to the dark and depressing diner was not high on his list, but his work there was not done.

Penny was curled up in her favorite booth, and he startled her out of her thoughts. Molly and Hank had worked past midnight to get the diner and catering orders all set, being sure they were ready for the day and free until the parade. Now, Penny was lost in her own thoughts about what her future might hold. Was it time to go? Was she living her life stuck in one big grave-like rut? She smoothed out her skirt and gave her ponytail an adjusting tug, preparing for whatever Jake had on his agenda for the final gasps of the night.

"I'm not surprised," she said. "You've made it pretty clear you can't stand it around here."

He could tell he had somehow offended her, and he stopped in the middle of the room.

"Hey, it's not so bad," he said, though he really didn't mean it. "There's just not much of anything to do on a regular basis—for us undead ghoulies, that is."

He moved around the counter and served himself a scoop of Rocky Road ice cream. The red glow of the emergency exit sign above the doorway behind him cast odd shadows across his face and left his already dark eyes black as coal.

Make yourself at home, she thought sarcastically, not even sure why he was annoying her so much tonight. Jake was who he was, and he wasn't behaving any differently than he did most nights.

"Where will you go?" she asked, trying to remember how his brazen behavior had charmed her in the past. "Fayetteville, for the college scene? Bikes, Blues, and Barbecue Weekend is coming in September. I bet you'll find all kinds of old-school biker ghosts around for that."

"Naw," Jake said, walking more calmly over to her booth, reminding himself that he still needed to charm her into the idea of going with him. "I'm thinkin' of heading north to the really big cities, where there are all kinds of things to see and do. Chicago. New York. Or south, maybe. I don't know for sure yet."

"Chicago?" Penny whispered. Her mind flashed images of tall buildings on the lake, evening concerts with her family, visiting the zoo at Lincoln Park, and taxis darting around busy city streets downtown. The image of her childhood house lingered in her memory.

"What about Chicago?" he said, hoping for a chink in her resolve.

"That's where I'm from, well, *way* back when."

Jake slid into the booth on the same side as Penny, forcing her to move her legs and put them under the table. No one ever came over onto her side of the booth. Even though she had grown accustomed to his constant closer-than-appropriate presence, he'd never been in this "sacred" space with her before. A few days earlier, it would have delighted her. Now it was just unnerving.

Jake's attempt at coaxing did not have the effect he'd hoped for. He offered her a bite of ice cream, but she just shook her head.

"Wouldn't you like to see the Windy City again?" he said, bumping his shoulder into hers.

"No, I would not," she responded firmly, shifting her body as far toward the wall as she could. "I'm sure it doesn't even look like the same place, and there's no one there anymore that I would know."

"Not even your sister? Maybe she had some kids and you are an auntie?" he continued, hoping to sway her.

"She doesn't live in Chicago," Penny said quietly.

Jake leaned back in surprise.

"And how do you know that?" he asked.

Penny shifted uncomfortably, remembering things that were easier left alone.

"Susie came through the diner, about twenty years ago, on a family vacation. I am an auntie. She has kids. Three of them, as a matter of fact. Two girls and a boy, who looks just like the pictures of our father when he was young. They were teenagers then. I remember thinking that she would be just shy of fifty years old. They all looked perfectly happy and content and just like any other family that comes through here."

"Well, what do you think about that?" Jake asked no one in particular. "How did you know it was her?"

"Molly always asks all kinds of questions when people come in. 'Where ya from? What ya seen? Having fun?' She got Susie talking about the last time she had been here, and the whole story spilled out about me and hoping for a cure but that I didn't make it. She never said my name, thank goodness. That might have made something click for Molly, and it could have really freaked her out. But it was enough for me. She still looked just like Susie. Taller and kind of rounder and more filled out, but still Susie. Her eyes were still exactly the same."

"So you just watched them eat?"

"I did. They all got cheeseburgers and shared blackberry cobbler a la mode for dessert. They chatted about the ghost tour at the Crescent and seeing the crazy fossil-covered walls at Quigley's Castle and wanting to visit a candy store before they left town that day. It was hard to see them go, but I was glad I got a glimpse into her life. They seemed really happy."

"Why didn't you follow them out?"

Penny sighed. It had certainly occurred to her. But watching them leave, all full of energy and life, she had wondered how it would really feel to witness their lives but never be a part of them. She had felt that enough around the diner, but it didn't matter with strangers.

"I thought about it," she admitted, "but what would be the point? Do I really want to haunt my sister? What if she could feel me around and it creeped her out?"

"What makes you think she'd notice you?"

"At one point, while they were here, Susie got a funny look on her face. Maybe she was just remembering coming to the diner back in the fifties as a family, but it seemed like there was more to it. She kind of looked around, like she was searching for something she could feel but not see. I was only a few feet away, standing close so I could hear them. I think she could sense me there."

Penny smiled, letting the memory of her little sister wash over her.

"Hmmm," Jake murmured. "No one living has noticed me, not even a little bit. Even when I poke 'em, they just swing around with no idea where I am."

"It might be a family thing. Where there were once bonds, I guess those don't just go away. Back when you were alive, didn't you ever feel someone looking at you or know someone had come in the room without having to look up?"

"No," he admitted, "I didn't."

"Well, I did," she continued. "I imagine it's the same kind of thing. Some people are more attuned to the world around them than others are."

Jake was pretty sure this was a bit of judgment being thrown in his direction, but he let it pass.

"Anyhow," Penny continued, "it was easier to just stay here. It was nice to have that moment and to see that she was happy and safe and has a wonderful family. That was enough."

"But that was twenty years ago."

"True," Penny said. "It was still enough."

Jake just shook his head. He couldn't understand how she kept so separate from life. Observing, but never diving in.

"There are things you have not learned about this afterlife stuff, Jake. If you think time flies for the living, multiply that by a thousand for the dead. It all just sort of blends together. Time doesn't pass the same way after a while. Days and weeks and months and even years just whiz by. You'll find you can kind of fast-forward things, zip through them, if you want. I learned to do that during the winter months when it is quiet around here. Walking through doors is not the only talent ghosts have."

The idea intrigued him, but confused him too.

"Why would you want to fast-forward through life?"

"Because it isn't *life* anymore, Jake. You don't have to sleep or eat or anything you don't want to do. You'll see. You've only been at this for a few weeks."

"Maybe, but not having to bother with eating and sleeping is the best part. Just go, go, go!"

"Ah, to be young," Penny sighed dramatically.

"I know, I know, you're an old lady," Jake said.

"Yes, a tired old lady in a poodle skirt and saddle shoes," she laughed.

"By the way, why doesn't that change?" Jake wondered aloud. "Your clothes, I mean. Silas is still wearing his convict clothes. Katie was stuck in her maid outfit, even though she hated being a maid and it's what killed her. I've got on riding boots I never even owned."

"I don't know, maybe it's just how I still see myself—how you see yourselves. I hear some of the most crinkly, hunched-over old ladies say that *inside* they still feel like girls. They sure giggle like them when they get to talking about being young over a bowl of ice cream."

Jake nodded. That made sense. He certainly didn't mind being stuck in his T-shirt, jeans, and riding gear. It was very much how he saw himself. And there was certainly nothing wrong with being twenty-one for all eternity.

"Maybe that's it," he said.

The faint braying of a donkey echoed down the hills and through the diner.

Hawww hee haw hee haaawww.

"It must be almost dawn," she determined. "The farmers are getting things up and moving."

Jake glanced out the window. The sun was just starting to peek over the hilltops. He could handle one more day in this town. It should be fun with the parade and parties to join later on. But what about after that?

It was clear now to Jake that Penny was never going to agree to leave with him. If her sister had not been able to lure her away, what hope did he have? Her afterlife here in this diner was too comfortable. She felt safe. She felt useful. She felt needed. And today she acted more annoyed with him than charmed. It would take a miracle to get her away, but it would be a shame to set out on his adventures without some female company. Who knew what worthwhile ghosts there might or might not be along the way? How could he convince her to go?

What if Molly and Hank were not so happy with having her around anymore? What if she caused trouble? Would they want her to leave? Of course, Penny would never actually cause them problems. But the living couldn't tell which ghost was making the mischief, could they?

What could he do quickly, he wondered, that was big enough to be unforgivable—to really get their attention—but that Penny couldn't clean up or explain away? One glance around the diner gave Jake his answer. It was so little and so simple.

"If you're really not going to come on an adventure to a big city, at least come up to Magnetic Spring with me before I go," he said calmly. "It's just up the street, barely a hundred yards, and it looks really amazing with the lights and decorations for the holiday weekend. Maybe we could even climb up on the rocks and watch the parade."

He saw a twinkle in Penny's eye.

"The parade?" she whispered. "I've only ever watched it through the window. So many people." She remembered parades from when she was a little girl, and her heart raced with delightful memories.

"If we get up on the rocks, we will have the best view in town and no one around us to have to worry about. Come on." He bumped his shoulder into her again, playfully. "Have some fun for once. Get in touch with that young girl inside you that still wears a ponytail and saddle shoes."

"Okay," she sighed. Then she straightened up tall. She'd crossed the street yesterday, and no harm was done. Watching the parade was a good start to getting out of her rut, and if he was really leaving that night, one short outing was called for. She could handle that much. It would be easy to get back to the diner if she was uncomfortable or felt unsafe. She suddenly felt fluttery inside, but in that great, something-wonderful-is-going-to-happen way. "Okay," she agreed more confidently. "Let's go see a parade."

"Excellent," he said, jumping up.

"But it doesn't start until almost lunchtime," she laughed.

"Oh, there's bound to be fun things to see before then. People will be setting up and fussing around. Let's go now and watch all of it."

Penny knew he was right. Nothing was going to happen in the diner until after the parade anyhow. Molly and Hank wouldn't even open up until right before it started. She shrugged and pulled herself out of the booth, and they both headed for the door, but then Jake stopped.

"Wait a sec," he said. "I need to take care of my bowl."

He thought it was a pretty good sign that Penny had been distracted enough by the potential field trip not to notice a dirty ice cream dish. His plan just might work.

"I'll get it," Penny said, starting back toward the table.

"No, no," he assured her quickly, "this is your day for some freedom. I can clean my own dish and put it away. I've seen you do it dozens of times. They'll never notice a spoon out of place."

"All right," she agreed with a laugh.

"Go enjoy the sunrise," he urged her. "I'll be out in just a minute."

Swishing her skirt from side to side happily, Penny waltzed out the front door.

Perfect, he thought.

Tough love. That's what his dad would have called it. Sometimes you had to do things that hurt folks to help them learn lessons and move on. In Jake's opinion, Penny most definitely needed to move on. She needed to wake up and start living again.

Time for Jake to step in.

Penny waited patiently outside, leaning on the fence railing and watching as the first rays of morning sun came up over the mountains— pink and orange and full of freshness and promise. Independence Day was always a special treat in this tourist town. Molly and Hank slept in late and opened the diner right before the parade to serve those waiting to watch out in front and from the garden. After it was done, dozens of visitors would flock in for the air conditioning and the ice cream. Maybe a burger, but mostly some nice cold ice cream or a soda.

Jake was true to his word and came out only a minute or two later, using the door so he didn't upset her.

"All set," he said.

"Lock the door behind you," Penny said in a happy, singsong voice.

"Yep," Jake said. *Lock it and leave it locked for hours. That should do it.*

Penny strode confidently to the corner of Magnetic and Main, then she waited for Jake.

"It's not far, you know," he laughed.

"I know," she smiled, "it's just been such a long time since I went any farther than this."

Jake offered up his arm, and Penny slipped hers through it. Then she walked courageously past the corner and up the hill to the festively decorated Magnetic Spring. She hadn't felt so free in years. Who was in a rut? Not her! She could be adventurous now and then and still not have to leave her diner behind for long. She would show them.

Behind her at the diner, Jake's plan was already in effect. It had only taken two shakes of a lamb's tail to set it in motion.

His dirty dish was still sitting on the table.

Chapter 11

Penny and Jake arrived at Magnetic Spring just as dawn gave way to the bright sun of morning, slanting between the trees and catching the edges of the craggy mountain walls that rose up on either side of the road. Main Street ran through one of the lowest sections of town, with the voluminous, rocky drainage well along the roadside, proving that this was where every drop of rain in Eureka Springs ran to in the end. In heavy storms, the culverts would overflow and leave the street looking more like a river than a road.

In direct contrast, Magnetic Road aimed straight up for higher ground, rising several hundred feet in its short span, twisting and curving along a natural path that had been traveled for centuries. In the winter, water would flow from the rocky mountainsides and freeze in beautiful formations. In the summer, it trickled down the sides slowly, ebbing and flowing around limestone juts, eroding the stony surface as it had for millions of years. Mosses and grasses took advantage of the moisture and grew along the rough walls. Not too far up the path, locals had sectioned off the area along the road where one of those magical springs burst forth in a natural cave in the side of the mountain. It had become a picnic spot and day-trip destination in the 1800s, and today it awaited Penny and Jake as they began the climb upward from the corner of Magnetic and Main.

The pair weren't in any rush to get up the mountain, and Penny was enjoying kicking small rocks along her path and running her fingers through the grass on the side of the mountain. As much as she had loved to lie in the soft grass of her backyard and stare up into the gently swaying trees when she was a little girl, she was shocked to realize that she had not actually touched a piece of grass since she had died.

She plucked a few thick stalks and held them together in-between her thumbs, the way her father had taught her, and tried blowing through them to make a whistling sound. It was even harder as a ghost than it had been as a child. All she got out of the grass was a desperate sputtering. Jake, of course, grabbed his own piece and immediately accomplished a shrill tweet that echoed off the rocky walls along the road.

Vivid memories of warm summer afternoons and picnics and a life of carefree abandon flooded Penny's thoughts—lying on the lawn for hours, watching butterflies and ladybugs. A glimpse of her father's shiny, brown, pointy-toed dress shoes, swooshing through the grass next to her when he got home from the office, flashed through her mind.

Closing her eyes, she could envision her father, a shock of black hair falling down over his forehead, bright red suspenders running up his chest, trying to demonstrate how to make grass whistle. *Papa.* Remembering him made her heart feel so full she thought it might burst, but in the best way possible. He would have been the first to drag her off to see a parade, that was for sure.

Jake was in a jolly mood too as he regaled Penny with all of the things he was going to see and do when he left town that night. He didn't once pester her about joining him. She was grateful for that and enjoyed just listening to his plans and laughing at the wildest ones. It was delightful to feel young and pretty and free from everything, basking in the glow of Jake's full attention. He might be a rascal, but he was a charming and handsome rascal, and Penny didn't see any reason not to enjoy his flattery for one more morning as they wound their way up to Magnetic Spring.

Eureka Springs was dotted with dozens of historical springs that boasted the flow of that same healing water that Penny had come to town to drink. Nobody drank directly from them anymore, but they still stood as lovely tourist attractions. Some of the springs had been built up with strong rock walls and gardens. Others were simpler and ignored. Magnetic Spring was one of the larger and more elaborate ones in town. It was also one of the most popular because it was right on a main road, with its own parking lot. It even boasted a covered picnic area and a trolley stop. Just pull right up and enjoy.

Penny thought it was the most beautiful thing she had ever seen. Standing in the empty lot, she gazed up the high mountain wall that contained the spring. It was surrounded by forest trees, manicured shrubs, and a beautiful bed of vibrant flowers—snapdragons and pink butterfly bushes, with impatiens and begonias at their feet. Off on the side of the steep incline sat huge limestone boulders with signs warning tourists not to climb on them—signs that were ignored daily. Children and adults could not resist the chance to feel like they were sitting on top of the world.

Today, in preparation for the holiday, American flags had been stuck in the ground where it was soft enough. Others hung from lampposts. There was a large red, white, and blue banner draped across the picnic area, and ribbons ran up and down posts and hung from every possible vantage point over the whole scene. Icicle Christmas lights were even hung on the picnic area to give it a twinkly glow. The whole spring was decorated from one end to the other.

Penny cheered at the festivity of it all and clapped her hands in glee. Then she ran up the stone steps to stand right at the foot of the spring bed. The water poured forth, as it had for centuries. Then she turned around and took in the view from up on the hillside.

Jake, sitting down below on a stone bench, just smiled at her and waved. He had never seen her look so full of energy and life. Maybe there was hope for her yet.

This is going to be much more fun than just watching from a window, she thought. She even contemplated making a habit of walking up to Magnetic Spring every Fourth of July. Or maybe she'd even go downtown to where the main stage was located and the groups would do their showing off to win prizes. She laughed at herself and shook her head. That was just Jake's ambitious talk clouding her thoughts. The reality of trying to navigate downtown on a day like this without bumping into the living was a different matter altogether. She'd never really do it. At least, not alone. Maybe she could if Jake came back to visit, or if Silas could be persuaded to use his skills at avoiding the living to escort her around.

Jake and Penny considered the different out-of-the-way-but-still-with-a-view locations to set up camp and decided to watch from atop the picnic area. The thin metal roof was not strong enough to hold anyone, so no one with actual weight would try to get up there. For those who no longer had a material body, weight was not a problem. They settled at the edge and let their legs hang down as just a few cars began to pass on Magnetic Road, headed toward Main Street.

Penny delighted in people-watching and witnessing elaborate floats chugging their way up the hill to get in line for the parade, swaying from side to side precariously, like they might fall apart at any moment. She and Jake chatted comfortably, and he sat shoulder to shoulder with her in a friendly, but not too pushy, way. It was perfect.

The parade started promptly at eleven o'clock a.m. The sun was already high in the summer sky by then. Penny could tell it was really hot and steamy for those who had gathered at the spring and along the roadside to watch the parade. They were fanning themselves and blotting sweat and drinking lots of water and soda to overcome the heat. Even those who set up umbrellas looked like they were cooking in the early July Ozark weather. At the far ends of the road, shimmers of heat masqueraded as puddles, but the parade participants marched right through them unsplashed.

Penny felt some warmth, just like she could sense that the sun was bright, but it didn't have the same detrimental effect on her as it did the living. She was happy for Hank and Molly that all of these hot and thirsty folks would be right near the diner as soon as the parade was over. It should be a really good day for them.

For over an hour, bands of all shapes and sizes, heavily-laden floats, decorated cars, high-stepping horses, and clowns throwing candy meandered past them. The marching band from Berryville strutted by to "Yankee Doodle," and interns from Turpentine Creek smiled through whisker-painted faces and fluffy tiger costumes.

They must be roasting! she thought.

Penny marveled at the spectacle of a hot-pink sports car pulling a float of a giant, plaster cheetah that was ridden by a beautiful woman in full Wonder Woman patriotic attire. To top it off, the Amazon had bright-red hair, and she hooted and hollered and waved and cheered, twirling a golden lasso, making the crowds go wild. Penny wished she could be so bold and daring.

But Penny's favorite part was the Shriners with their funny little red hats and their little cars, zipping all over the road, nearly crashing into each other and making the children cheer. It was all absolutely delightful. As every fire truck in town drove by, sirens blaring to signal the end of the parade, Penny clapped and cheered. Then she turned to smile at Jake.

"Thank you for getting me out here. This was a real treat."

"Promise me you'll get out of the diner more after I've hit the road. There are hundreds of ghosts in town. Don't wait for them to come visit you. Head out to see Silas on his mountain. It's really beautiful there. Wander into town and hit the Mud Street Cafe, or go to one of the bars in town to hear a band or two."

"A rock band?" she laughed. "That's a little loud for my style."

Jake just pshawed her away.

"Do it. You still have life here that you can do something with. Don't waste it sitting around that diner."

"But I like sitting around that diner," Penny said, suddenly deflated. It had been so nice to just be, without all of his nagging. "Don't spoil a perfectly good morning, Jake. This is a wonderful little town. You might appreciate it more if you just tried."

"Sorry, sorry." He threw up his hands in defeat. "No more about it, I promise."

"Thank you," she said, smoothing her skirt and looking back down at the happy families. Each was now packing up chairs and coolers. A few loaded their things into nearby cars, but almost all of them were heading down the road toward her very own Magnetic Diner.

Excellent! Penny thought.

"Let's head down to see how things are going," she said.

He nodded and smiled, but he knew what must be already unfolding down at her beloved diner.

Sorry, Penny, he thought. *Really, it's for the best. You'll see.*

He was fully prepared for the fact that she wouldn't see it that way.

Chapter 12

Penny and Jake hung back from the crowd as they strolled slowly down the hill toward the diner. Penny was simply enjoying the energy from the happy people and the sunshine and the beautiful day. Jake was encouraging her delays. He was in no hurry to get back. The longer it took, the better. These might be the last moments she ever spoke to him for all eternity if his plan backfired, but "ya don't win big, if you don't risk big." That's what his pa always said.

Jake could see evidence that his efforts had been effective before they even made it to the corner. As the two ghosts neared the bend in the road, Jake noticed that families were already turning to come back up the hill. A young mother carrying a crying toddler caught his eye.

"It's okay," the mother said, "there are other places in town we can get ice cream."

That caught Penny's attention too. She froze in her tracks and watched the mother and child walk by, the toddler kicking his heels in frustration. Then another sad-looking family. And another.

"But Mom," a little boy whined, pulling at her arm, "we always go *there*!"

"I know, I know." The mother shook her head. "Every year since I was little. But this year they had to close."

CLOSE?

Penny felt a chill pass through her, colder than a waft from the freezer on a hot summer day. Why would the diner be closed? Was something wrong with Molly or Hank?

"Oh, Jake," she whispered, "something horrible has happened. I just know it. They would never close early, today of all days."

Jake tried to act nonchalant and unconcerned, even while he knew that Penny's afterlife would never be the same. The first part of his agenda had worked.

"I'm sure it's nothing. Maybe they just wanted a holiday, like everyone else."

Penny stared at him blankly, certain that was the stupidest thing anyone had ever said. Clearly, Jake had never run a diner and had no idea how to make money with one. *Close on the Fourth of July? Seriously?*

"No," Penny said, trying not to let her renewed irritation with him show. She headed for the side of the road to avoid the crowd. "Something is terribly wrong."

The pair struggled against the tide of tired paradegoers. Everyone had turned around, and all of the families, young and old, were heading back up the hill to their cars, empty-handed. When Penny and Jake reached the diner, the street and garden around it were deserted. No cars in the parking lot. No line waiting for ice cream.

Penny ran for the front door, but she found it locked up tight. The "Closed" sign was flipped into place, but the lights were on inside. Through the windows in the door, Penny could see Molly sitting at the counter with her head in her hands. Hank was behind the counter, leaning down and talking to her. At least they were both okay.

Only one option lay before her. Unless she wanted to wait until the owners left and try to slip in then, Penny would have to go through the door. Moving through objects was the most horrible feeling in the world to Penny. It was like the screeching sound a fork made when it hit a plate wrong—like fingernails on a blackboard. No real damage done, but she hated it anyhow.

Waiting to get in would mean not hearing what was being said right then. There was clearly a problem. It looked like Molly was crying, and Hank was frowning deeply. It reminded her of that sad day years ago when Molly had found out she couldn't have children. But even through all of the grief, they'd never missed a day of work. What could be so awful that it would make them close down the diner?

Penny gathered her courage, sucked in her breath, and pushed her way through the door. *Ugh!* she shuddered on the other side. Her whole being tingled with the revolting sensation of trying to take up the same space as a material object. She couldn't understand how other ghosts did that all the time.

Shaking it off, she saw that she was right. Molly was crying and had been really sobbing hard earlier, based on the pile of Kleenex on the counter next to her. Jake appeared at Penny's side a moment later, clearly unfazed by his walk through the wall.

Does anything bother him? she wondered.

Everything in the diner seemed to be in place, but immediately Penny noticed that it felt odd inside. It took her a minute to translate the feeling. Hot. Stuffy. The diner never felt like that.

Is the air conditioning broken? That would be inconvenient, for sure, but that didn't seem enough of a reason to close or for Molly to be crying. It was the kind of thing she would laugh off. She'd open the windows to try to get a breeze and do business anyhow. The customers would just take their ice cream and go.

The phone rang, breaking her questioning thoughts and startling Molly and Hank. Instead of moving to the phone, Molly just put her head down on the counter and folded her arms over it. Hank sighed and answered the call.

"Magnetic Diner," he said flatly, with none of the charm and spark that usually went into greeting a caller. "Yes, it's true," he responded to the person on the line. "Of course, we will refund everything you've already paid. We just don't know how long the food wasn't properly refrigerated, so we can't serve any of it. Sandra is scrambling at her place and trying to make up most of the catering orders for us. Do you have her number? . . . Good. Just give her a call and let her know what you need for the day. Again, I'm so sorry. I hope your party goes well. Thanks."

Hank hung up the phone and plopped down on a nearby stool.

"I think that was the last one," he said to Molly. "I'll go double-check the books and make sure we didn't miss getting in touch with somebody."

Hank got up and headed into the office. As he moved the red-checked curtain aside to pass, Penny gasped in horror. Nothing had been moved since Hank and Molly had walked into the diner late that morning, but it was not at all how Penny had left it. The giant metal refrigerator and freezer doors sat propped wide open. A wooden doorstop was wedged firmly and purposefully under each. Just inside the door to the freezer, Penny could see puddles of ice cream on the floor. Pools of pink, blue, and brown oozed together as they lazily headed for the drain in the floor.

"Oh, no," she whispered, dread settling in her stomach like a rock.

Before she even got to the ice cream display case, Penny could see that the lid was up. Inside, her fears were confirmed. Nothing but brown-and-cream-colored tubs of liquid. Everything was melted.

Hank came back out, and Molly looked up at him with a tear-stained face. A blast of cold air whooshed across Penny from the vent above her head.

"We've talked to everyone who had a catering order in for the day," Hank assured his wife. "So at least that's done. I turned the air back on so we don't roast while we get all of this cleaned up."

Cold air? So it's not broken. Then why was it so hot in here?

Penny couldn't imagine what had happened between the time she walked out of the diner and right now. It didn't make any sense. Looking around in confusion, she saw Jake's ice cream bowl still on the table at the corner booth.

Didn't he say he would clean that up? Isn't that why he stayed inside?

Penny spun around to ask him, but Jake had vanished.

Like the bright sun rising that morning, the reality of what must have happened—what Jake must have done when he went back inside—dawned on Penny. If she were alive, she would have been sick. Now all she could do was clutch her middle and crumple against the wall. The feelings were still the same.

Does he think this is a joke? Was this supposed to be funny—a prank that we would laugh about?

Penny looked up at Molly and saw that she had turned from the counter and was staring at the bowl across the room, sitting alone on the table at the corner booth. She didn't seem terribly surprised to see it there, as if she had always suspected something like that went on behind her back. Hank had already headed toward the freezer.

"Be careful lifting those ice cream tubs out of the display," he said. "We can just dump them in the sink back here. I'll pull in the big garbage cans. It's all going to have to go."

Molly looked from the corner booth and gazed around the room, as if searching for whoever might have left the bowl there. She considered saying something aloud, but stopped and grimaced. Then she pulled herself from the stool and began the long, depressing task of cleaning up the mess left behind from Jake's antics.

Penny watched in despair as five-gallon tub after five-gallon tub of Blue Bell Ice Cream was poured down the drain. Tuna salad and hamburger patties and piles of other ingredients were pulled from the cooler and tossed into the trash. Without knowing how long the food had been left without refrigeration, there was no other choice. Large platters of prepared sandwiches and bowls of potato salad were unceremoniously dumped.

She had heard the couple talk enough about inventory and catering events to know that thousands of dollars' worth of food and work was now nothing more than a pile of trash. Income that they counted on to get them through the tourist-free winter months was gone. The pain deep in her stomach only grew worse the more she thought about it.

By the time it was over and the floors were cleaned, the sun was sinking low in the sky. Since it was a holiday, it was impossible to place orders for more food until tomorrow. They would be unable to open until more ice cream and supplies arrived. It was as if a dark cloud had settled over the diner and sucked away the joys and excitement from that morning.

"I can run by and grab some of the basics at Hart's tomorrow morning so we can at least do some burgers and stuff," Hank mumbled as he flopped down at the counter when the cleanup was complete. "That can hold us for a day or two of lunch and dinner service."

With nothing more to be done, the exhausted and depressed couple simply locked up and went home. As Molly shut the front door behind her, she paused for a moment and looked back into the room. Often, when she did this, she would say something to Penny. The ghost had not moved from her spot on the wall. Now she waited to see what Molly would say, but apparently, there was nothing to say. In the end, Molly just sighed, nodded her head, and locked the door firmly behind her.

Nearly despondent, Penny turned to seek the comfort of her favorite corner booth, but there, on the table, Jake's dirty dish still sat. Hank probably hadn't noticed it. Molly probably didn't want to touch it. Penny couldn't face it. She burst into tears.

Chapter 13

When Penny was all cried out, she forced herself to go to the corner booth and clean up Jake's dirty bowl. The least she could do was make sure Molly didn't have to deal with it when she came back in the morning. Penny washed and soaped and dried everything he might have come into contact with, as if she could scrub away what had happened to her friends in the process.

As beautiful as the day had been, storm clouds blew in with the darkness of night. They now rumbled and threatened in the sky all around. At first Penny thought it was the fireworks on Holiday Island, which was surprising since it was too far away to see or hear them, especially down in her valley. Once it began to pour, she just hoped the show hadn't been rained out. At least some people should get to have a pleasant end to their holiday.

Penny curled up sideways in her favorite booth, her knees tucked up under her chin, and helplessly listened to the wind and rain battering against the windows. Try as she might, Penny could not fully grasp why in the world Jake had played such a prank on her friends. All the clues pointed to him. His immediate disappearance from the scene sealed his guilt. He had often shown himself to be selfish, reckless, and thoughtless, but not downright cruel. The harsh reality of what he was capable of was more than she could fathom.

It was now late in the evening, and the storm was still raging, so Penny was surprised to hear voices out in front of the diner. She listened for a moment, thinking it could be Jake or Silas, but she distinguished Hank and Molly, talking animatedly with a familiar male voice. A moment later, the front door flew open, and the couple rushed in, followed by Sheriff Jimmy. Hank closed his huge umbrella and shook it out onto the mat at the door. He and Molly peeled off their wet raincoats, but Sheriff Jimmy just lowered the hood on his, dripping streams of water down his back.

He entered slowly, despite the weather, running his gloved fingers along the door lock and the frame around the opening, examining for evidence.

"It would've been better if you'd left everythin' just as it was," he said. "There might have been a clue or two as to who was here."

Hank hovered near the cash register, but Molly walked straight over to the corner booth and stood at the end of the table. Penny was surprised to have Molly come toward her with such intent. She dropped her feet under the table to sit properly, half expecting Molly to join her, but the woman just stared at the table, hands on her hips, at the spot where she had left Jake's bowl. It was now gone. She let out a frustrated snort and turned back to face Jimmy.

"We weren't even going to call you," she said, "but we realized that what little of the damage our insurance may cover will require some kind of police report."

"Don't ya worry so much about the money. Pine Mountain Theater is already figuring out how to have a fundraiser for ya. This town takes care of its own, so don't ya fuss about that. But why in the world wouldn't ya report someone breakin' in and ruinin' yer stuff?" Jimmy asked.

Molly and Hank exchanged glances. Molly raised an eyebrow, but Hank just shook his head sadly. After originally finding the vandalism and a lengthy discussion in the privacy of their own home, there was only one conclusion the couple could reach.

"No one broke in," Hank said quietly.

"What say?"

"No one broke in. The door was locked. It's not a complicated lock, just like the front door of our house, but it's still a good, solid lock. There was no sign of anyone getting in through the windows or door by force. We don't have any hidden keys. Only Molly and I have a key, so no one got in that way." He paused, shifting his feet uncomfortably. "It would have to be someone who doesn't need to open the door to get in."

Jimmy looked questioningly from one of the pair to the other, then a knowing look crossed his face and he nodded. Molly and Hank nodded back.

"So it's like that, is it?" Jimmy said.

"We think so," Molly said as she sat glumly on a stool at the counter. "There really isn't any other explanation."

"But how can ya be sure?"

Molly looked at the ground. Hank didn't say anything.

"Molly," Jimmy pressed, "now's the time ta tell me. Heavens ta Betsy, ya know I've heard it *all* over the years. Not much is gonna shock me."

Molly looked up and stared blankly at her old friend.

"I know, Jimmy," she whispered. "We just never talk about it out loud. Things about ghosts and spirits around this building that we've known since I was a teenager, long before we owned this place, we just don't talk about it." Molly's shoulders slumped, and she sighed, long past tired.

Before she owned the place? Penny wondered in shock. *Before they married? She knew I was here long before that?*

"So something like this has happened before?" Jimmy asked in surprise.

"No." Molly shook her head. "Nothing even remotely like this. I'm not even sure she's here all the time. I called out to her when we discovered the mess and tried to get her to write something on the chalkboard for me, but she didn't answer. Some days I can feel her around. Other days I don't. Penny is quiet and well-behaved, and we never even really notice her."

"Penny?"

"Yes."

"Ya know its name?" he asked, a bit horrified at the idea.

"Yes."

"It writes on the blackboard?" he said.

"Yes, she has written on it once or twice."

They all stood quietly for a moment while the sheriff absorbed this new information. Jimmy was pensive. Penny felt the knot return to her stomach.

They knew she hung around the diner. Molly could feel her—had felt her long before Penny realized—but that was not the worst part of what Penny was beginning to understand. Hank and Molly thought she had something to do with what had happened that day. Molly had even tried to ask her about it, but she had been off gallivanting with Jake and had given no answer. Penny had been absent when Molly needed her, and it broke her heart. The knot in her stomach moved up into her chest, and tears of sorrow started again. *I never should have gone to the parade. Never should have left the diner.*

"We haven't had any trouble from her," Molly continued. "Not even the slightest bit. Sometimes I would notice things not quite in place, or some items missing from the freezer when we did inventory, but never any damage or pranks or trouble like you hear from other places in town."

Jimmy looked around the diner hesitantly.

"We have had a lot of odd reports in the last few weeks," he admitted. "Lots of things that don't add up to anything logical. Probably a bunch more that I could lump in there too, if I wanted to. Lots of stolen motorcycles with the keys in them and bar fights that no one admits to starting and stores with display windows rearranged."

Jimmy looked at Hank, and Hank just shrugged.

"I find it all a bit hard to swallow," Hank said. "There didn't seem to be much harm in having a ghost around. It wasn't too big a deal. Even if I noticed somethin' weird, I figured there was always some other explanation. But . . ." Hank looked at Molly. She nodded, encouraging him. "When we came late this morning to open up for the parade, there was a dirty ice cream bowl on the table over there."

They all turned and looked right at Penny. Her blood ran cold as they all stared at her, but didn't see her. *Hank noticed the bowl.*

"The day before a holiday rush, you know we didn't leave a dirty dish just sittin' on a table," Hank continued. "We make extra sure that everythin' is locked up tight, sparkling clean, and ready for the day. So how did that bowl get there?"

Jimmy adjusted his police jacket uncomfortably.

"Did ya notice anything funny about the bowl when ya cleaned it up?"

"I didn't clean it up," Hank said.

Jimmy looked at Molly. She shook her head.

"I didn't clean it up either," she said. "I was so angry that I didn't want to touch it. When we came back in with you . . ." She motioned at the clean table.

"Well, at least ya have a ghost who's willin' to tidy up," he offered.

"After trashing the place," Hank added.

Molly grimaced, and Penny wished she had left the bowl where it was.

"So ya think yer ghost left the refrigerator and freezer doors propped open and opened the ice cream display case and turned off the air conditioning?" Jimmy clarified.

Molly just shrugged.

"It doesn't make any sense after all of these years," she admitted, "but I'm not sure what else to think. I've never noticed any other ghosts around but her."

They think I did this, Penny thought in despair. *They think I ruined their business and cost them thousands of dollars.*

"Ya know, there's a solution to troublesome ghosts that stick around too long," Jimmy said.

The three of them looked at each other carefully. Hank nodded slowly. Molly pursed her lips. Jimmy measured their responses.

What solution? Penny wondered, pretty sure she would not like the answer.

"Everyone in town knows about the solution," Molly finally admitted. "Her house is only a mile up the road."

"Well, then?" Jimmy said.

"We've never really worried about it," Molly admitted. "Lots of places in town have their ghosts to deal with."

"Or make money off of," Hank added.

"Penny minds her own business," Molly said, "and I often forget she is around at all. Nothing like this has ever happened before."

Hank cleared his throat and looked at his shoes.

"What is it, Hank?" Molly asked.

"It creeps me out," he said.

"What?"

"Wondering if there's a ghost in here creeps me out. I hate coming over here alone. Once I had to come back and check something in the office after closing, and the place had a really strange feeling. Like there were lots of them here. I told myself it's only my imagination, but it still gives me the willies."

Penny remembered that night. Yes, there had been several ghosts here, but Hank had never shown any sign of noticing.

I creep him out, Penny acknowledged sadly. That had never occurred to her.

"Maybe there were lots of them here last night, and they had a little party," Jimmy suggested.

"Happy Independence Day," Hank said sarcastically.

"It just doesn't make sense," Molly sighed. "I've never felt anything but comfort from Penny's presence. At some of my darkest times, it felt like she was sitting right next to me."

I was, Penny thought. She pulled her knees up tightly against her chest again. *I was always there. I never left you alone, except today.*

Hank sat down next to Molly and took her hands.

"Maybe, just maybe, that is what you felt because you needed to feel that. Not because it was real."

Molly's shoulders slunched and she wrapped her arms around her middle, but she nodded slightly.

"It sure felt real."

Hank put his arms around her, and Jimmy fidgeted with his jacket, pretending to look for something in the pockets. Finally, Molly straightened up and looked Hank in the eye.

"Fine," she said quietly. "Do it."

Penny sensed that this was the end of a very long conversation. Molly was sad and resigned, but Hank jumped up immediately.

"I'll call her now," he said. Then he looked around the diner hesitantly. "I'll call from the house," he concluded. Molly, Jimmy, and Penny watched as Hank sprinted from the diner without even grabbing his raincoat or umbrella.

Once he left the building, Molly didn't seem so confident. She leaned her elbows on her lap and stared down at her shoes. Penny considered moving toward her to offer some comfort, as she would have in the past, but somehow she wasn't sure that making Molly aware of her presence would be helpful tonight. She would find a way to talk to her after the sheriff left. She would head to the chalkboard and try to explain it all. She didn't really want to write anything in front of Jimmy. There would be time later.

Before Penny had too long to consider it further, Silas burst through the wall near the front door and looked around excitedly. Spotting Penny, he swooshed across the room—a motion ghosts normally just used for long-distance travel. Startled, Penny cringed back to the far side of her booth. She'd never seen Silas so animated and wild-eyed.

"Do it be true?" he asked her in bewilderment.

"Is what true?"

"Did dat crazy fella gets in here an' make all kinda mess?"

"Yes," she admitted. "Jake's not around to ask, but he was in here alone. When they came in to open up, the freezer doors had been propped open, and all of the food was ruined."

"Now, what he be goin' and doin' somethin' crazy like dat fer?" Silas said, sitting down across the booth from Penny.

Penny just shook her head. She didn't understand why Jake did most of the things he did around town. Her only guess was that he liked it. The way he died, flying off that mountain, led her to believe that he'd probably been troublesome when he was alive too. Handsome and charming, even deep and thoughtful sometimes, but troublesome.

Silas looked over at Molly. She was now just sitting in silence, like she was waiting for something. Rain battered at the windows, but she was oblivious to it.

"How did you know what happened?" Penny asked.

"Up on my mountain, dey be havin' a weddin' today," he explained. "Da diner was suppozed to has all da food ready fer a hundred guests. Dey be all fussin' and fumin' and runnin' 'round like crazy folk, tryin' ta find somewheres else ta gets it. Da food showed up in da end. I didn' catch everythin' dey say, but it sound bad, so I comes ta see ya. I figure dey be gone by now."

"Oh, that's terrible. I heard Hank on the phone talking to someone about canceling their order. I was so worried about things here, I didn't stop to think about what would be happening at all the parties and weddings around town that were counting on Molly and Hank to provide food for them. What a mess."

"Do dey tink it be robbers, or jus some teenage prankstas?" Silas asked.

"No," Penny said, "they are very confident that it was ghosts."

Silas leaned back in his seat in wonder, eyes wide.

"Well, I'll be," he exclaimed. "What's Jimmy tink abouts dat?"

"He believes them," she said.

Silas shook his head and made a *tsk tsk tsk* sound.

"They think it was me, or that I had something to do with it," she admitted, smoothing her skirt and trying not to cry again.

"So," he continued, "what is dey gonna do abouts it?"

"I'm not sure," Penny said, "but Hank left to make a phone call."

"Who he callin'?"

"I don't know, but they all agreed it was a solution. They talked about calling *her*, and that she was right up the road. Maybe someone they can get supplies from?"

Silas's eyes got wider, and he sucked in a deep breath.

"What?" Penny asked, now a bit frightened, but Hank came back through the front door before Silas could answer. He shook the rain from his hair and stomped his boots on the mat.

"She's on her way," he said, his voice rising with excitement.

Molly stood up and clung to the chair back.

"Right now?" she asked. "In this storm?"

"I thought she might beat me here."

"Who's coming?" Penny asked, looking at Silas. His expression had changed from surprise to one of pure, unadulterated horror. "Who, Silas? What are they talking about?"

"Tell 'em ya didn' do it," he whispered in a panic, leaning across the table and grabbing both of her hands in his. Silas had never touched her before, and it shot vibrations of electric terror up both of her arms. "Write somethin' on da chalkboard. No, too lates now. We gots to go, now, an' never come back."

"Silas, I can't leave now. I have to explain what happened."

"Oh, Lordy. She's a-comin'. I can feel it in my bones. I cain't stay here!" Silas yelled wildly. "I sorry, Miss Penny," he whispered again. "Try nots ta fight too much. Dey say dat makes it harder. I never forgets ya, not ever."

And with that, Silas burst through the wall right next to them, out into the blustery night beyond.

"Silas?" Penny yelled after him. "What's happening?"

Penny's question was left hanging in the air as the front door swung open wildly. The tempestuous winds whooshed through the diner, bringing with them a crazy twirl of strawberry-blonde hair and billowy, dark-purple fabric. Slamming the door behind her, the visitor leaned against it for a moment, blue eyes ablaze. Shaking off droplets of water that rolled easily away, she attempted to smooth her windblown mane.

Moving purposefully away from the door and adjusting her dozen or so necklaces, each one dripping with a magical crystal or ornamental fairy, Angelina the Magnificent made it clear that she now owned the room. Penny shrunk into the corner of her booth, her mouth agape.

Her? They called HER?

"Where is she?" Angelina demanded, her bright eyes flashing. "I haven't come out on a night like this to trifle with tourist shenanigans."

Hank and Molly hesitated, but they knew it was too late to back out now. Angelina had been called, and she would not leave without Penny.

Chapter 14

Everyone in town knew about Angelina the Magnificent. A city famous for its ghost stories and legends always had a medium or two ready to help out those who were not so fond of the dead-but-not-gone occupants of their homes and businesses. Angelina the Magnificent was who you called when you wanted a ghost gone, and she had proven her talents effective from one end of the earth to the other.

She was no exorcist, there was no church involved, but Angelina knew a thing or two about talking to ghosts and moving them on their way. She used crystals and meditation and candlelit vigils, but mostly she called on an inherent power deep inside of herself. It was a talent that had been passed down for generations through the women in her family. Some had kept it quiet, but others had celebrated it, and Angelina took great pride in her ability to aid both lost souls and the people haunted by them. She might have earned her living reading tarot cards and auras for tourists in a quaint little shop on Main Street, but her real talent was communing with the dead. She was a legacy, and she was an expert. No soul had ever escaped her.

As Penny watched the medium stride regally across the diner, she fully expected to see the glass fairies around Angelina's neck spring into life and dance around her in the air. A magical aura radiated from her, filling the room with that same electricity that The Light had brought the night Katie left. Maybe Silas was right, Penny thought. She should run and never look back, but she found that she couldn't move or even think clearly. It was like a nightmare come to life. It wasn't possible.

Molly and Hank have called Angelina the Magnificent to remove me.

The reality of this moment was more than Penny could fully process. She had heard the stories, horrible stories, about happy ghosts being forcibly removed from their favorite spots by Angelina. Even hearing Molly and Hank talk about ways to handle problem ghosts, and that they were calling "her," Penny had never in a million years imagined that she would be face-to-face with the medium. Angelina meant serious business. There would be no smoke or mirrors or trickery. When Angelina came for a ghost, that ghost left, one way or another.

Penny considered making a dash for the chalkboard to try to write something, anything, that could change Molly's mind, but she felt glued to her spot. Never in all of her years had Penny felt a force as strong as this medium. The storm raged outside, but Penny felt the ominous presence of an even greater force of nature right inside her dear little diner. The wind and lightning and thunder didn't hold a candle to the power the medium had in her arsenal.

"Where is she?" Angelina the Magnificent asked again, looking pointedly at Molly.

"I'm not sure. She may be here right now," Molly whispered. "We can't see her."

"Penny, is it?" Angelina asked.

Molly nodded.

"Penny?" the medium demanded in a forceful, brass voice. "Are you with us now?"

Not used to being addressed directly by strangers, Penny wasn't sure what to say.

Now in the middle of the room, the medium suddenly froze, and a wild look came over her face. Angelina straightened her arms dramatically, flexing her ring-covered fingers, tipped with long, ruby-red nails. Then, slowly, she began to raise her arms up at her sides, the long sleeves of her purple robe fanning out beside her. Everyone in the diner sat just as rooted in place, waiting. The living were not aware of the vibrant field of energy spreading slowly through the diner, but Penny felt it wash over her like a wave. She was enveloped in a calmness, but there was also a demanding, questioning nature to the feeling running through her and around her.

When Angelina the Magnificent finally reached a point where her arms were shoulder level and stretched taut, she threw back her head, hair flying, and demanded with the full, compelling strength of her powers, "Answer me now, Penny!"

As if it was dragged from deep within her, Penny yelled, "I'm right here!" Then she clapped her hands over her mouth. Never in her life had anyone made her do something outside of her free will, but she was completely helpless—held in the grip of the medium's power.

Angelina spun to face her, both arms now stretched out to the exact spot where Penny sat, curled up in her favorite corner booth, the medium's long fingers pointing the way.

Molly gasped and clutched at Hank's arm.

"Oh, don't hurt her," she whispered.

Angelina took a lurching, zombie-like step toward Penny.

Scared by her wild behavior, Penny contemplated running again, but she still couldn't move from her spot. Silas had warned her not to fight. Maybe that would just make the medium angry.

What will happen if she gets angry? Penny shuddered.

"You do not need to fear me, Penny," Angelina said, her eyes open wide, arms stretched out. "I am only here to help you find your way."

"No," Penny answered, "I don't need your help."

Angelina's head twitched, as if she had heard.

Maybe the medium would leave her alone if she could just understand what had happened. Penny wasn't a ghost that needed to be removed. She was kind and peaceful and kept to herself. The diner was where she belonged, and she had to help Angelina see that.

"Your friends here are worried about you, Penny. They want me to help you to move on to the next stage of your life journey."

Angelina's arms relaxed a bit, but her eyes were still focused on the spot where Penny sat. Her gaze bored right though Penny, questioning and searching.

"They don't need to worry," Penny answered. "I didn't cause any of this trouble, I swear. This is where I'm supposed to be. I help others like me. I need to be here. This is my home."

The medium suddenly relaxed. Her eyes stayed focused but lost their wildness. Eyebrows furrowed, Angelina walked slowly across the room and slid tentatively into the booth across from Penny. She closed her eyes and dramatically placed both of her hands on the table between them, with just the tips of her fingers touching the surface. The red from her nails blended perfectly with the tabletop and seemed to become one with it. Inches from Penny, Angelina communed with unseen forces.

Penny could feel the vibrations come through the table, up her legs from the floor, and right through the red, vinyl seat of her booth. Her being was encircled in the energy of the medium's presence. Penny's thoughts echoed with whispered questions. She closed her eyes, unable to resist the tender probings.

Who are you? Why are you here? Why do you stay in this diner? Penny wasn't consciously aware of giving any direct answers, but she sensed that Angelina was finding them in her own way.

Finally, Angelina sighed and lowered her head, releasing Penny, who fell onto the seat back behind her.

"So much loss. So much sadness. So much . . ." The medium raised her head, like she was testing the air around her, searching for just the right word. "So much . . . so much . . . *responsibility*," she sighed.

Angelina reached out a hand to Molly, still standing across the room and holding Hank's arm in a death grip. Molly released him and tiptoed hesitantly to the side of the booth. The medium grabbed her hand firmly.

"Tell her she can go," Angelina demanded. "Tell her that it is okay to go. She needs to hear it from you."

"What?" Molly said, stunned.

"Tell her she can go," the medium repeated. "Tell her now and be firm and clear."

Molly cleared her throat and looked around the room. Hank nodded to encourage her.

"Penny," Molly said quietly, looking more at the table than where Penny actually sat. "Penny, you can go on now. It's okay."

"Oh, Molly," Penny said, hoping she could be understood, "you don't have to worry about me. I'm just fine. No problem. I don't need to go."

Molly might not have understood, but Angelina did. She lurched up and slammed both hands flat on the table in front of her, eyes wild again and focused on Molly.

"Free her, Molly!" she yelled. "Free her now!"

"I don't know . . ." Molly stammered. "Maybe we are being too hasty. What if it wasn't Penny who caused all the trouble? It could have been another ghost. We don't need to do this."

"None of that matters now. She needs to be free. Tell her to go! Tell her to get out!"

"Oh, Angelina, we were just upset and scared, we don't need to—"

"*Now!*" the medium yelled, flashing the full intensity of her stare on Molly.

Angelina leapt from the booth, her strawberry hair whipping across her face uncontained, and grabbed both of Molly's hands violently. Lightning flashed in the windows, sending eerie bolts of light across both of their faces. Thunder crashed, rattling the walls and the Coca-Cola glasses on the shelves.

"Set. Her. Free," she whispered slowly and clearly into Molly's horrified face. "DO IT!!"

Angelina closed her eyes and threw back her head, her mane of hair flying. Another wave of psychic electricity rolled through the diner, bouncing off the Coca-Cola wallpaper and flying from the red ceiling fans. Penny felt every hair on her body stand on end as she watched Molly's eyes grow wider. Angelina glared back down at the woman, whose knees buckled, her whole being filled with the power and intensity of Angelina's gaze.

"Get out!" Molly yelled in one impelled gasp. "Penny, we don't want you here. Get out now!"

Penny was shocked, but she knew Molly was just doing what she was told.

"Oh, Molly," Penny said, pushing in desperation past the vibrations that hummed in the air. "I won't leave you. We can just pretend to make her happy. It will all be okay."

Angelina jerked her head back toward Penny like she had heard a gunshot. Then she yanked on Molly's arms.

"Again, and mean it! In your heart, you have to set her free!" she growled.

"*Get out!*" Molly yelled louder, caught in the power of the medium's grip. "We are sick of having you here, always around, even if we can't see you. It's scary and it's wrong and you don't belong here. *Go!*" Molly shouted, but tears began to roll down her cheeks.

"Tell her you don't need her!"

Molly sobbed, but she complied.

"We don't need you here. Go, Penny. *Go!*"

Angelina threw her hands up into the air, releasing Molly, who collapsed onto the floor and buried her face in her hands, sobs wracking her body. Penny wanted to run to her, but she suddenly felt an energy race through the diner that was stronger than any life force she had ever felt. Stronger than a group of delighted senior citizens. Stronger than a preschooler who had spent the day watching tigers and lions. Stronger than newlyweds on their honeymoon. It was such a strong force that it had an actual brightness to it.

Angelina smiled and reached out toward Penny.

"Yes!" she yelled. "Say *yes*, Penny!"

The Light reflected off the crystals around Angelina's neck. It bounced back from a Coca-Cola mirror on the wall. It filled Penny with warmth and peace.

"It's safe, Penny!" the medium encouraged. "Let go! No more responsibility here! Release it all!"

She moved toward Penny, arms open in a wide embrace.

Penny felt the pull, felt The Light filling her. It was soft and calm and promised a new beginning. She started to look toward it, but fear gripped her like an icy hand on her shoulder. If she let this happen, there would be no turning back. Molly would think she had destroyed their holiday. Silas would worry about her. Jake would never know what had happened. All those poor souls who came through the diner would have no one to help them. She couldn't go. Not yet.

"NO!" Penny yelled in a passionate sob as she jumped from her spot in the corner booth, finally wrenching free from Angelina's mental hold. "No!"

The brightness vanished, snapped off like a light switch. Angelina gasped and spun around wildly.

Running to the middle of the room, Penny didn't know where to turn. Molly was curled up on the floor crying, and Hank had rushed over to comfort her. Jimmy was frozen in shock. Angelina twirled madly, hair and robes and necklaces flying, searching the room for a sense of Penny's presence. Turning away from that scene, Penny saw Jake standing outside the door. He smiled at her through the glass and nodded.

Penny knew now that her days of comfort here in her diner were over. Whatever the cause, whatever explanations she might be able to write on that chalkboard, none of it mattered now. Molly and Hank had wanted her gone so badly they had called in Angelina the Magnificent. They had called in a medium to get rid of their ghost. She would never feel safe and comfortable and welcome there again.

"Penny?" Angelina called urgently. "Penny?"

Penny walked slowly but resolutely toward the door. Jake pushed it open with a slam that startled everyone in the room, and Penny, chin held high, walked out past him—out into the world. Then Jake let the screen slam behind them.

Molly stared at the door through her tears.

"Penny?" she whispered.

Angelina sighed and arranged her dress and necklaces. "She left."

"Will she be back?" Hank asked.

Angelina paused, listening.

"I can't be sure," she admitted. "She did not go on as she should have. I am certain of that, but she has taken a first step. She has let go a little bit."

Hank helped Molly up into the booth. Wiping away tears, Molly put her hand tenderly on the spot where Penny had been.

"Oh, Penny," she whispered. "I'm so sorry."

Angelina spun around in anger.

"No, don't be sorry. Don't pull her back in. Penny is just as stuck as any other ghost. Helping her stay stuck is not a kindness."

Molly smiled weakly and nodded. She understood, but it didn't help her feel less guilty for yelling at Penny and sending her away.

"We never had any children, you know?" she said sadly. "Just knowing Penny was around somehow made that more bearable." Hank slid into the booth next to her and held her hands gently.

"And she felt that pull," Angelina said, her voice tinged with annoyance. "I guarantee it. She felt that as a responsibility to you and this diner. I've never felt such a heavy burden of false responsibility in my life. Your loneliness was not her problem to solve. Don't keep her chained to this place. You have to make her go."

Then she softened some and sat down across from Molly and Hank.

"Children are not supposed to stay tucked away at home forever, no matter how comfortable and safe it is. They need to move forward, but it can be scary. Sometimes the mother bird has to shove the babies out of the nest so they can begin the next stage of their lives. They are scared to fly, but they must. It is the next step and the natural progress of their existence. Penny needed a shove. She needs to fly now. She needs her new life to start."

Molly nodded. She understood, but it didn't help. She dropped her head onto the table and sobbed.

Chapter 15

Once Penny had walked out the door, right past Jake, she did not stop until she hit the corner. In the darkness, puddles glistened and shone in the moonlight. The rain had ended, but the warm summer wind still whipped the trees around like they were feathers. Flashes of lightning and low rumbles of answering thunder echoed through the valley. Everything was damp and drippy. Bits of water flew off the willow tree branches as the gusts twisted and turned them. Not really being a part of any of it, Penny didn't feel it. All she felt was a grief that ached in her heart. Standing at the crossroads of Magnetic and Main, Penny wasn't sure what came next.

"You didn't keep your promise, you know," Jake said from behind her.

"What?" she said, without turning around.

"We promised each other that if The Light came again we would pay attention to it."

She smiled weakly.

"I didn't look. You're right. I knew what might happen if I looked, and I didn't want to leave. That must have been enough to end it."

Jake moved to the very edge of the sidewalk, his toes touching the line where the concrete walkway met the asphalt of the road. He raised his arms out to the sides and pointed in opposite directions, like the Scarecrow in *The Wizard of Oz*.

"So, where now?" he asked, full of anticipation.

Penny couldn't even fathom that question. She looked back at the diner. From where she was standing, she couldn't see in any windows to tell what was happening inside after her dramatic departure. The medium had not emerged yet.

"How can I really go?" she said.

"Well, it's kinda rude to stay," he laughed. "Molly was pretty clear."

"I know, but she didn't mean it. Not really. They were just upset about what you did."

Penny turned to face him.

"Wait . . . Why would you do such a horrible thing to them?" she asked, frustrated anger rising back up. "Don't try to deny it. I know it was you, but I can't understand it at all. Did you think it was funny?"

Jake shrugged and looked down at his feet, tracing the edge of the sidewalk with his boot.

"It is a huge deal, not just some little prank. They lost tons of money and upset so many people, and now they are angry with me and sent me away."

Then it hit her, and she felt a boulder settle in her stomach. She was standing outside the diner, shunned from the place she loved, because of what he had done. That had been his plan all along. If he couldn't convince her to leave with him, he would force her hand.

"Oh," was all she could say when faced with the cold, hard facts. She knew she should be furious, but she just didn't have the energy for that much more emotion. At least it finally made some sense. He wasn't intentionally cruel, she realized that. He was just the most selfish, immature person she had ever met, and Jake would continue to do whatever he felt like doing, whenever he felt like doing it, for a long time to come.

She knew she should yell at him and rage about how he hurt her friends and ruined her life, but it all seemed pointless. He'd never understand. Standing at the dark corner, Penny just felt pity for him. How could anyone without compassion truly love or be loved? One day he would learn. She hoped that with every fiber of her being, but she had no intention of being part of his life for the next fifty years while he figured it out.

"It's for the best, really it is," Jake said sheepishly. "Molly and Hank will recover, and now you are free to get on with your life."

"I had an amazing life," she sighed, emotional exhaustion settling in. "For over sixty years. There were people who needed me, and I was able to help them. Not just Molly. So many lost souls coming through that diner. So scared. I can help. I'm going to have to find a way to watch for them. Molly and Hank won't notice me if I only come in at night. Then I can keep helping those poor people move on."

Jake stared up the road into the darkness for a minute, considering his words carefully. He had already shattered her comfortable world this far, so he decided that he might as well finish the job.

"Penny, if you are really honest about it, how many of those people would have found their way just fine without you?"

"What do you mean?"

"I mean, you take on all this sense of personal obligation to help the recently dead find their way along, but isn't that something that happens naturally 99.9 percent of the time? And the ones who get stuck, like me, you can't really stop that from happening, can you?"

Penny considered this. Of all the hundreds of transitional souls that she had encountered over the years, how many genuinely couldn't have made it without her? She moved from the corner and sat down on the bright-yellow flower box surrounding the "Magnetic Ice Cream" sign to honestly judge the answer. Had she really mattered to any of them?

"Now don't get all anxious and stressed out," Jake said. "I'm not saying you didn't make things nice for them, but was it really a vital service, like you seem to think it was? Would they be stuck if you weren't there, or would they go on just the same when The Light came for them?"

"I don't know," she whispered, the truth of it all settling heavily in her heart. "I felt like they needed me, but maybe it wasn't true at all."

Jake sat down next to her.

"Remember when we talked about the day you died? You said that you thought you didn't go on the first time because you felt like your sister needed you. She was begging you to stay, so you did."

Penny nodded. Yes, that was the conclusion she had reached.

"But you *didn't* stay with her," Jake continued, growing more animated. "You ended up here."

Penny considered this too. She had only seen her sister once since the day she died.

"You thought you stayed to support your sister because you thought she'd be lost without you, but she turned out just fine."

It was true. Penny had to admit it. She had ended up stuck, but it hadn't benefited her sister at all. Susie had still grown up sibling-less. There was nothing Penny had been able to do to change it.

"I don't believe that you need to sneak back into the diner every night to save whoever shows up. You've got to let that go, Penny, just like you've got to let Molly go. None of it is your responsibility."

The idea that everyone would be just fine without her was a sobering one. She did her best to help care for the potential ghosts who came through the diner, but it was true that most of the time they just moved on effortlessly when The Light came for them. She certainly hadn't figured out any magical way to help those poor ones who fought The Light and got stuck. They were just as stuck, with or without a bowl of ice cream in front of them.

But what about Katie? She had been stuck for over a century, but then she was gone in the snap of a finger. What had happened there? Had she made a difference to Katie? Or was it the other way around? Had Katie made a difference for Penny—given her the proof of how and why The Light could come again?

"It's time to go now," Jake said, breaking her thoughts. "There's no reason to stay any longer."

Glancing around the garden, Penny drank in every bit of her favorite place on earth. The willow tree and the diner and the town full of wonderful people and ghosts. She realized that the wind had calmed, and everything was now wet, but still. The storm had passed. At least the one that had raged outside. Inside, Penny still felt a wreck of confusion, but one truth was crystal clear to her.

"No," Penny said calmly.

"What do you mean *no*?" he laughed. "Are you just gonna keep sittin' here outside the diner? They don't want you in there anymore, Penny."

"Maybe, maybe not," she admitted. "But I'm not going with you either way."

Jake huffed in frustration. This was not how his plan was supposed to go.

But Penny had already come to terms with her decision before they trotted off to the parade. Jake was handsome and delightful and charming and fun, but a ghostly, mischief-filled life with him was not in the cards. Not for her. If there had been any unconscious wavering, his prank had only served to wipe away any last doubts. It should be flattering, how much time and energy this young man had devoted to capturing her attention, but a huge part of her didn't even understand why he was so insistent for her company.

"Jake," she finally asked, "while we are being all up-front and honest here, why do you want me to come with you so badly? What is it about me that makes it worth all of the fuss and bother?"

Would he fall down on one knee and profess his undying love for her? Penny was pretty sure, even if he did, that he wouldn't mean it. It would be just another ploy to persuade her.

Jake met her eyes, those same sparkling, emerald eyes that he had found himself facing the night he'd appeared in the diner. The night he had died.

She was beautiful, that was an easy answer, but he knew it was a pathetic one. Certainly there was more to it than that. But when he thought hard about it, Jake wasn't sure why it was so important. Was he so in love with her that he couldn't live without her? No, it was nothing that deep. Did he need her company? Well, he'd been having a great time around town without her. Was it just the challenge he couldn't resist?

"We really don't have anything in common, you know," she continued. "I understand that you look at me and see a young girl, but you know that's not quite true."

"A very pretty young girl," he added with a charming smile.

"Maybe so," she laughed.

"With amazing green eyes," he teased, leaning in close.

"Okay, okay." She squirmed and pushed him away, embarrassed. No one had fussed about her looks since she was a little girl, and the people around her these days couldn't see her. Flattery was not going to get him what he wanted this time. She was not going to fall back into her girly behavior and succumb to his charms and make foolish decisions. It was time to wake up and face the cold, hard facts of her afterlife.

"Think about all the things you want to get away from in this town and what you want to do. Do you think any of that is appealing to me?"

"No, I suppose not," he admitted.

"You need to let this go," she said. "Maybe you just feel attached to me in the same way that I have felt attached to this diner. I was there for you in a desperate moment of your existence. That's an important bond between us that will never be broken. But it doesn't mean that I should leave with you, or that you really want me to be with you every minute of every day for years upon years to come."

Jake considered this. *Every minute of every day?*

"I certainly would never allow you to go into ladies' lingerie stores and make trouble."

"Well, that would be a great loss," he laughed. "I have several of those stops on my agenda."

"Oh, Jake, heaven help the city that ends up with you haunting it."

"What makes you think there will only be one?" he joked, and she rolled her eyes at the thought of it.

"I must admit, though," Penny sighed, "you have brought more excitement into my life than anything in the last sixty years. Maybe more. And I will miss hearing your stories. It will be boring for the local police around here without your daily antics."

"I only wanted what is best for you, Penny," he said earnestly, taking her hand into his one last time. "You know that, don't you? I don't always go about things the right way, I know—I never have—but I just wanted you to be free and live and find happiness. I want you to get out of that diner and find out what more there is in the world for you. I still want that for you, even if it isn't with me. Are you sure about staying here?"

Penny nodded and squeezed his hand. Even if she didn't agree with how he went about things, his heart was in the right place. Looking at this young man from the vantage point of a woman of eighty, envisioning herself more as his mother or grandmother, she could imagine his potential—the man he could become. She had witnessed glimpses of it. He had eternity ahead to figure it all out. She really was going to miss him, in many ways. Everyone else had talked at her. Jake had asked her questions—questions that had changed her whole outlook—and listened to her answers.

"Do you believe me? I never meant to hurt you," he worried.

"I do. And I will be fine. There is plenty to do in this town and hundreds of ghosts I can turn to. You can go away on your own, Jake, and everything will be okay," she said. "Go and live and try not to make too much trouble. They may call in Angelina the Magnificent for you yet."

The mention of her name reminded Jake that the medium was still just a stone's throw away, right inside the diner. He didn't much like being this close to someone who might open up that portal to the afterworld for him. Not just yet, at least.

With one last look at Penny, who smiled encouragingly, Jake released her hand, stood up, adjusted his leather jacket, gave a quick nod of agreement, and stuffed his hands into his pockets.

"Where will you go first?" she asked.

"New Orleans, baby!" he said. "I hear there's all kinds of supernatural action down that way. If I head over to Harrison, I can take Highway 7 all the way down to the Louisiana border. There's plenty of stories of ghosts along that route, so no one will much care about anything I might do."

"Stay safe," she said. "Maybe we will run into each other again sometime, if you come back this way."

Not sure what else to do, he bent over and gave Penny a kiss on the forehead. It tingled with gentle affection. Then, with a mischievous grin, he disappeared.

Good luck, Jake, she thought with a smile.

Now she was left alone with her own future to consider. She would miss the attention he lavished on her—how beautiful and special he made her feel—but looking back on it now, Penny wasn't so sure it had ever been genuine. Jake liked to be charming. He liked the chase. Maybe she'd even made it more interesting by keeping him at arm's length. Jake the Rake, indeed.

But he didn't really need her—didn't really love her. Not the way she longed to be loved and needed. His presence in her life had awakened that natural longing to be part of a relationship, to be valued and cherished. She couldn't go back to being simply seventeen and naïve, head over heels for the class clown, but she could hope for love, couldn't she? That twinkle Katie had in her eye right before she left, that's what Penny wanted to feel. That's what she had been longing for all of those years in the diner, and she hadn't even realized it.

Rising from the flower box, Penny considered her options. Looking toward the diner, she yearned to go back inside and curl up in her safe corner booth. But how many more years would she pass just sitting there? She could go back to visit, but there was now a gulf of disappointment between Penny and her former haunting grounds. All of that time, all of those people and decades passing by, and Penny was still ultimately alone. Molly was not her family, as much as both of them might have wanted that to be true. The souls who showed up at night could find their own way, she admitted that now too. It was, finally, time to discover how her life would unfold if she was willing to let it.

Looking around from the corner of Magnetic and Main, Penny had no clue what direction to venture first. Gazing up the road toward Magnetic Spring, that route seemed the safest place to start. She had just been there that morning and knew what to expect. It might even be a comforting and familiar place to begin.

Wandering past the corner, Penny stopped at the old U-shaped thong tree at the side of the road next to the mailbox for 1 Magnetic Drive. She had heard Donna talk about the historical significance of those trees, how the Native Americans in the area had bent young saplings to help mark their trails and find water. There was certainly plenty of water all around, so it must have stood as a way-finding mark, right here at the start of Magnetic Road. Her new life could begin along this ancient trail.

Am I on the right path? she silently asked those ancient travelers. *Is there a way to be part of a family again? To love and be truly loved?*

As the bright moonlight began to break through the clouds, Penny followed the road, back up the mountain to where she had so happily watched the Independence Day parade just a few hours before. Had it only been a day? Time was often blurry for a ghost, but this day had been a whopper.

Independence Day, Penny thought as she trudged slowly up the road, making the climb toward Magnetic Spring. *Is it a day for my freedom too?*

Chapter 16

The sheriff left the diner, scratching his head and muttering about what to file in his report, leaving Angelina to sit with Molly while she regained her composure. Hank made his rounds, closing things down for the night—making absolutely sure the freezer and refrigerator doors were firmly closed—and then the three of them headed out the front door. The wind had become nothing more than a gentle breeze. Moonlight covered the front garden, glancing between the old willow tree branches, and everything was peaceful and calm.

With a quiet "Goodnight," Molly and Hank headed over to their own simple house, but Angelina hesitated on the porch of the diner. This evening had not transpired how she had expected.

When a ghost was stuck and The Light came for it, Angelina could feel it and knew that everything would be all right. The energy that filled the room left her tingling for days, and she was assured that her powers had been used for amazing good—helping a lost soul find his or her way along on the journey of life. The living who they left behind were also enveloped by the peaceful energy. There was a joyful sense of accomplishment and fulfillment. The medium had experienced that same euphoria in Italy, in France, in Africa, and everywhere else in the world where she had traveled and shared her gift.

This night had not felt like that. It had started out well. Angelina had felt the buzz and pull and electricity in the room, but then it had all gone wrong. Denial, resistance, obligation, fear—that was all she had sensed in the end. It also seemed to be what Molly and Hank were left with. Resignation, but no true peace.

Angelina watched the couple as they headed up the sidewalk, but behind her she suddenly experienced that vibration in the fabric of the air that always signaled the presence of someone who no longer belonged. Gasping, she turned to face up the sidewalk, toward the corner of Magnetic and Main, where the diner's welcoming sign stood. Was Penny still around? This presence felt larger than just her.

Walking slowly in the direction where she had felt the echoes of life, Angelina wondered if she might get a second chance. Breathing deep into the center of her being, Angelina mentally reached out to whoever was there. Unconsciously, she raised both of her arms, stretching out to find answers.

Molly had heard the medium gasp and stopped in her tracks. She and Hank now stood frozen on the sidewalk behind Angelina, watching. Her motions were just like what had happened in the diner that evening.

Is Penny still here? Molly wondered.

She wanted to ask—to call out to Penny—but she thought better of it. Molly understood now what needed to happen. It was one of the hardest things she had ever had to do, but she understood. Shove the baby bird from the nest. A dear soul like Penny, who had brought her so much comfort, deserved to have a full future, free from the confines of their diner. Hank could be as skeptical as he wanted, but Molly knew what she had felt over the years. Now it was time to set Penny free.

Angelina the Magnificent walked slowly all the way to the corner, searching earnestly for Penny's presence. Then she turned toward Magnetic Spring. The energy was even stronger in that direction. Slowly and carefully, Angelina climbed up the road, oblivious as the billowing edges of her purple gown dragged through puddles. The rocky mountainside glistened with streams of water in the moonlight. Frogs croaked rhythmically in harmony with the katydids and cicadas, but the medium ignored all of it. She was totally focused, and tracing

Penny's journey had her full attention. Molly and Hank followed, keeping their distance.

When Angelina reached the spring, she used all of the power at her disposal to search for Penny. It was obvious to the medium that she was there. Was she hiding? Upset?

"Penny?" she called out softly.

Penny had not noticed Angelina coming up the hill. The confused ghost was simply sitting on the stone wall out in front of the elaborately decorated spring. She had been watching some rainwater drain down the side of the wall, changing its course around rocks and moss, but never ceasing in its travels. It was the kind of thing she hadn't witnessed in so many years. After being cooped up inside all the time, the simple pleasures of rain and its quiet remnants were a delightful distraction from her worries.

This time, Penny didn't feel any fear over the woman with the crazy jewelry and wild, strawberry hair. Everything felt more intimate and personal and relaxed.

"Penny?" she said again, nearly whispering. "Will you let me talk to you?"

"Yes," Penny said aloud. Angelina had heard her earlier, so why not now?

The medium slowly turned her gaze closer to where Penny was sitting, her eyebrows furrowed, as if she was not quite sure if she was imagining the feelings or actually sensing the ghost there.

"You don't have anything to fear, you know," Angelina said.

Do I fear whatever is in The Light? Penny pondered that. *No,* she concluded. It wasn't really fear of what was in The Light. It was just fear of leaving all of this behind, fear of moving on, fear of the unknown. Now that she sat out in the open, her life in limbo, the future didn't seem so fraught with trepidation. At the time when she should be most frightened, Penny felt tranquil. She had let go of so much that day, and she had survived. Life continued to be life. She just needed to discover her new place in the rhythm of existence as it flowed around and through her.

She closed her eyes and remembered the look on Katie's face right before she vanished. No, Katie hadn't looked afraid. She had looked elated. Totally joyful. Relieved. They all had. So many of them, over so many dozens of years. No one ever looked frightened when they gazed into The Light. So many faces filled with peace and joy and happiness.

I wouldn't mind feeling like that, Penny thought.

Angelina tilted her head, as if she could comprehend Penny's thoughts as clearly as her spoken words.

"If you are not scared, and you think you are ready, I can help you. That's what I do. I help people who got lost in their life-journey to find their way along."

Penny had to laugh to herself. That was what she thought *she* did too.

"If you are really ready, the first thing you need to do is let go. Just put down all the responsibility you feel for everyone and everything here. You can't take that baggage with you. Those concerns are no longer yours. Staying here, worrying and fussing about this life, has never been the plan for you."

The plan? Penny wondered. All these years, she had concluded that being at home in the diner was what she was supposed to be doing. She had felt so helpful and needed, but now she could see that the medium was right. This indeterminate state of existence—not really alive, but not really dead-and-gone either—was never the plan for her. She had been stuck as much as any other ghost in town. How could being stuck ever be right?

"I'm not sure why you ended up at the diner in the first place, but I know why you stayed. I can feel it deep in my bones. A heavy, heavy sense of duty and obligation. Such a desperate need for love and acknowledgment. So much love you have, but so much worry too. Now is the time to put all of that down."

Penny agreed. It was time to leave behind the charming diner with the Coca-Cola signs and fans and wallpaper. Time to say goodbye to the bright-red counter top where she had served so many bowls of ice cream and listened to Molly try to solve everyone else's problems. Time to walk away from the safe corner booth where she had watched the living world go by. It was time to leave behind people whom she loved but couldn't really communicate with—who couldn't really love her in return. She could wander around the mortal world for decades more, looking for another home and family, or she could just give in, like she should have in 1952.

It is time.

Taking a deep breath, Penny did her best to let it all go—to clear her mind of Molly and all of the people who might show up at the diner in the days to come. The universe would take care of them all just fine. She had to let them go.

But what about poor Silas? Penny remembered his face before he fled the diner that night. Poor frightened and alone Silas. Had he ever known a day of contentment?

"Who?" the medium asked, sensing Penny's thoughts and worry.

Penny climbed down from the rock and picked up a stick nearby. In the dirt of the flower bed, she wrote "Silas" and then "Serenity Mountain."

Angelina watched in shock as the message was scrawled out in front of her. It looked like childish chicken scratch, but she could read the words. She had never heard of a Silas in town, so it must be about another ghost.

"Penny, is this another lost soul? Do you want me to help him? I can go there first thing in the morning and find him."

Penny drew a smiley face in the dirt. Yes, Angelina would help him. He would be safe. It wouldn't be easy, but now that the medium knew he was there, Penny was sure she would keep searching until she found him. Silas could move on too.

"It's okay, Penny. Everyone here is going to be just fine. You can let go. Say goodbye."

Closing her eyes, Penny imagined each of them smiling at her—Molly and Jake and Silas—and waving goodbye.

They all have their own journeys to walk, and so do I. They will all be just fine. With a deep sigh, Penny released it all.

A surge of vibrant energy filled the air around her. When Penny opened her eyes, the opening of Magnetic Spring was filled with a brilliant glowing Light that shone down through the night. It should have been blinding, or blazing hot like the sun on a summer day at the beach, but instead it felt soft and gentle and full of grace.

Angelina clapped her hands over her mouth, refusing the temptation to say or do anything more. There was no way she was going to interrupt this magical moment. This was one of those amazingly rare times—one of those universally spiritual events that the women in her family had spoken of but the medium had never experienced for herself. A cosmic blessing, where she was perfectly in tune with the ghostly presence at hand.

Angelina could see The Light, and in the glow of that radiance, she could see Penny too.

Turning away from Angelina, Penny started slowly up the staircase toward Magnetic Spring. At the top, The Light grew even brighter, like it was pouring forth from the spring itself. Finally, Penny was ready for the glorious energy of a calling that was just for her. It was full of calmness and love.

Watching in silent awe from the shadows of the parking lot, Molly and Hank witnessed The Light too, and a young woman in a blue poodle skirt, her dark ponytail swaying gently from side to side as she climbed the steps toward the spring.

It was real, Molly realized. *It was all one hundred percent real.*

"Goodbye, Penny," Molly barely whispered, as Hank grasped her hand.

Sitting silently on the roof of the picnic area, in the same spot he had shared with Penny only a few hours before, Jake smiled. He couldn't really leave until he was sure she was safe. He'd been hovering out of sight, watching. It might not be time for him yet, but he had to admit that Penny was right where she was supposed to be. It was time for her to leave—he'd been right about that, at least. Time for her to move on.

"See ya later," he sighed.

From the shadows across the street, Silas watched as well. He wasn't going to reveal himself with the medium still so close by, but he had been observing from a distance to see what would happen to his friend. She was safe, he was assured of that now, and he also had proof that The Light could come again. He couldn't hear what Penny and Angelina had talked about, but he could tell she was not afraid of the medium. Maybe the rumors had been wrong. As he watched Penny's face, Silas knew there was nothing to fear. Maybe his time would come soon too.

But Penny didn't notice any of them. She had absolutely released them and left that part of her life behind. Gazing straight ahead, staring fully into The Light, Penny opened her heart to the path that lay before her. Within The Light, two figures emerged, and she could see the faint outline of others behind them. The pull became so strong that there was nothing else.

Love. Penny was enveloped in love.

"Mama? Papa?" Penny wondered aloud.

Then she was gone.

- The End -

Gratitude and Author Notes

Publishing this book would not have been possible without the support and encouragement of my husband, Scott. He often took over my household chores, along with his own, so that I would have time to write—or just went outside to play and left me alone with Penny and my thoughts.

I must also give credit to fellow author Angela Sage Larsen (creator of both the Petalwink and the Fifties Chix book series, www.angelasagelarsen.com). Reading a Facebook post about a diner that we had visited "at the corner of Magnetic and Main," she commented that this would make a great book title. That was all it took to get my imagination going. You never know where a little spark will take you. The first scene that I wrote included Angelina the Magnificent, in my friend's honor.

This story would not be in quite the same form without early and imperative intervention by The Queen of Damn Good Advice, my dear friend Annette Bridges (www.annettebridges.com). As the second reader of an early manuscript (my husband always being the first), she agreed with me that Penny and Jake needed more of a love story of some sort. But her take on it was different than mine and exactly what the story required. Jake should shake Penny out of the spiritless existence she has fallen into.

Even though they end up moving in different directions, as tends to happen in many real-life love stories, it is okay because they have helped each other to develop and grow. It may not have been true and lasting love for Penny and Jake, but it certainly woke her up to the possibilities of a fuller and freer life.

Many thanks also go out to my other beta readers: Kristi Reigle, Earleen Bailey, and Chris Raymond. I so appreciated your thoughts along the way.

And unending gratitude to Duke and Kimberly Pennell for agreeing to take a chance on me and this book, and for all their work to make it beautiful.

If you visit my town, you will find that the Eureka Springs of this story is a fictionalized version of the quaint, small town, but if you visit the corner of Magnetic and Main, you will find a delightful diner with Coca-Cola wallpaper.

My family moved to Eureka Springs the summer of 2012, purchasing property and setting it up as a guest house and wedding venue. It was delightful to watch how this book unfolded and began to include some of the local things that we love so much about this town.

If you visit in the summer, you will most likely be woken up by braying donkeys or mules. They live with the herds of cows to help keep the calves safe (cows are domesticated, not wild, and do not have the instinct to defend their young from coyotes and other dangers). Just below our property is grazing land, and their donkeys can often be heard echoing across our mountaintop. We call it "donkey o'clock," which often comes at five o'clock a.m.

You may also notice, if you take a van tour of the city, that your guide's fancy costume may remind you of someone in the story. If you are riding with Miss Savilatea Grace deChorum, then you have met the inspiration for Donna. We saw her at a ribbon cutting for the new putt-putt course during our first month in town, dressed from head to toe in white lace, and I thought, "What's up with that?" We learned quickly. Her van tours are delightful. Donna is my own creation, but no one from town would miss the connection.

I should add a disclaimer that the real Fourth of July parade route in town does not come anywhere near the corner of Magnetic and Main. The dozens of parades held in town each year (there are *lots* of them) all come down Spring Street, through the heart of the historic downtown area. I'm sure the local shops prefer it that way. When the first draft of this book was written, I had not actually been to a Eureka

Springs July Fourth parade, so the written version came purely from my desires and imagination. Wonder Woman, you know who you are.

Shriners darting around in their little cars and ending the parade with blaring fire engines may not take place in Eureka Springs (or any other town in 2014 for that matter), but they are strong memories for me of childhood July Fourth parades in Champaign-Urbana, Illinois, and evoked that feeling of small-town America that I wanted Penny to be experiencing. Those parades are one of the few vivid, tactile memories from my youth. Everyone should experience a small-town parade at least once in her life.

I hope reading this book will inspire you to make a trip through the Ozark Mountains and maybe even visit Eureka Springs. If you do, be sure to heed the posted speed limit and warning signs, especially if you are on a motorcycle.

Appendix

Many of the places and events in this story are based on historical information or local attractions in Eureka Springs, Arkansas. Here are some behind-the-scenes details.

Eureka Springs: This small city in Northwest Arkansas was actually founded by people seeking healing from its magical waters in the 1880s. Even the Native Americans in the area thought the "Great Healing Spring" held special powers. There are more than sixty springs in town. Magnetic Spring is lovely and is right where this book says it is—just east of the corner of Magnetic and Main. The entire downtown area is listed in the National Register of Historic Places. You can find out more at www.eurekasprings.org.

Ice Cream Delights: This is the shop that was the inspiration for Magnetic Ice Cream Parlor and Diner. My husband and I visited there for lunch one day shortly after we moved to town while we were investigating local places. The apple dumplings are amazing. As in the story, it is covered in Coca-Cola memorabilia. It is owned by a lovely couple, but I don't know them and did not base the characters of Molly and Hank on them or their lives.

Turpentine Creek Wildlife Refuge: This is a real place just outside of Eureka Springs. My family loves to visit and volunteer there, and I became a docent in 2014. For over twenty years, their goal has been "To provide lifetime refuge for abandoned, abused, and neglected 'Big Cats' with emphasis on Tigers, Lions, Leopards, and Cougars." At the time of publication, they housed over 130 animals, including bears like Bam Bam the grizzly and two "ligers"—a mix of a lion and a tiger. You can find out more at www.turpentinecreek.org.

The Crescent Hotel: In the book, this haunted hotel is the home of the Irish ghost, Katie. Founded in 1886, the Crescent is registered as a Historic Hotel of America. Known as "America's Most Haunted Hotel," it runs nightly ghost tours and many plays and events annually for ghost hunters and enthusiasts, including the Eureka Springs Paranormal Weekend. Check out www.crescent-hotel.com.

Quigley's Castle: One of Eureka Springs' quirkiest tourist attractions, this house was built out of rocks found right on the property. Read the whole story at www.quigleyscastle.com.

Mud Street: The original main street back in the 1880s, this road was so muddy that it earned its name. As the city has settled and sunk and concrete roads were built up, businesses that were once at street level are now below ground. Visit one of my favorite places, the Mud Street Cafe, to enjoy some amazing hot chocolate and dine below what is now Main Street. You can find them at www.mudstreetcafe.com.

The Fine Art of Romance: This is the real lingerie shop where I imagined Jake stirring up some trouble. The owners, Kelly and Leslie, and the manager, Lilah, were some of the kindest and most welcoming people we met when we first moved to town. While I was working on this book, they made huge renovations to the store, including adding wonderful dressing rooms with wood doors. Much to his dismay, Jake would not be able to blow the curtains open now. You can order your foundation wear and much more at www.fineartofromance.com.

The Great Passion Play: As the name would suggest, this Eureka Springs cornerstone tourist spot involves dramatizations of the Passion of the Christ, but it is also home to a Bible exhibit and other attractions, as well as the Christ of the Ozarks statue. You can find more information at www.greatpassionplay.org.

The Oregon Trail: If you did not study this in school like Penny did, it's a time in American history worth looking into. As many as twenty-one thousand people are estimated to have died along the trail for various reasons. The character of Katie would have made the journey much later than most, when railway service was established, but with no money, she would not have been able to afford the train ride. By 1890-1900, only poor immigrants were consistently using the trail route on foot. Having a strong Irish heritage myself, and growing up with stories about my grandparents running in a land race around 1893 to get their Oklahoma turf, Katie and her experience are close to my heart.

Bluebird or Serenity Mountain: The scene of a Jake-instigated bar fight and Silas's home, the high spot just east of Eureka Springs—at around 1,400 feet—was really the home of a biker bar and hotel, as well as a rental guest house called Serenity Hilltop Retreat across the street. That property has a cave where convict road workers were rumored to stay in the 1920s. There have not been any actual reported ghost sightings, so far. You can find out more at www.serenityhilltop.com.

Blue Bell Ice Cream: This special brand from Brenham, Texas, is actually what is served at Ice Cream Delights, and that especially caught our attention when we moved here since we had lived only an hour away from the factory. If you are ever in Brenham, be sure to take a factory tour. Whatever crazy flavor they are offering, I'm sure it's worth a try.

Thong Trees: These are historical treasures. It is true that Native Americans bent and shaped young trees to force them to grow in a special U shape to mark trails and water sources, as well as locations of caves and medicinal herbs. At the time of this writing, one stands just a few yards from the corner of Magnetic and Main. Arkansas is the name of a Native tribe, but local trees were probably formed by the Osage.

Shriners: Also known as the Ancient Arabic Order of the Nobles of the Mystic Shrine, this branch of Freemasonry dates back to 1870. Despite how the name sounds, it was originally a fraternity of stoneworking professionals, not a religious order (though members must believe in a Supreme Being). I learned that I would be eligible to join one of the women's chapters because my great-grandfather was a Freemason (the Grand Secretary of the Blue Lodge in Oklahoma) until the day he died. Find out more for yourself at www.shrinershq.org.

Highway 62: This road does run through Eureka Springs and over Bluebird or Serenity Mountain, as the story depicts, and it is full of dangerous hairpin turns. It was built around 1920 by convicts (like the fictional Silas), who lived in camps along the way. When we purchased our property, we were told that, while the section of road in front of our house was being built, the convicts stayed in the cave area on-site. I cannot definitely confirm this rumor, but it is possible. Highway 62 runs from the Mexico-US border in El Paso all the way to the Canada-US border in Niagara Falls.

Highway 7: Considered to have more ghosts per mile than any highway in America, this road—filled with hairpin turns—runs through nearly all of the state of Arkansas. You may be able to find the book *Ghosts of Arkansas Highway #7* by Gary Weibye through your local library.

About Meg

Meg Dendler has considered herself a writer since she won a picture book contest in 5th grade and entertained her classmates with ongoing sequels for the rest of the year. Beginning serious work as a freelancer in the '90s while teaching elementary and middle school, Meg has over one hundred articles in print, including interviews with Kirk Douglas, Sylvester Stallone, and Dwayne "The Rock" Johnson. She has won contests with her short stories and poetry, along with multiple international awards for her best-selling "Cats in the Mirror" alien rescue cat children's book series. *At the Corner of Magnetic and Main* is her first adult novel, but it won't be her last.

Meg and her family live in Northwest Arkansas. Visit her at **www.MegDendler.com** for more information about upcoming books and events and all of Meg's social media links.

Dear Reader,
If you enjoyed this
book enough to review
it for Goodreads, B&N,
or Amazon.com, I'd
appreciate it!
Thanks, Meg

Find more great reads at
Pen-L.com